The Childhood of a Spy

THE CHILDHOOD OF A SPY

BY DONNA GOOLD

Copyright © 2021 Donna Goold
The right of Donna Goold to be recognised as the creator of this original work has been asserted. All rights reserved. No part of this book may be reproduced or used in any manner without the prior written permission of the copyright owner, except for the use of brief quotations in a book review.

Disclaimer

This is a work of fiction. Unless otherwise indicated, all the names, characters, businesses, places, events, and incidents in this book are either the product of the author's imagination or used in a fictitious manner. Any resemblance to actual persons, living or dead, or actual events is purely coincidental.

Cover art by Scott Tetlow
Edited by Helen Baggott
Layout by Oliver Tooley
Printed by Severn, Gloucester
Cover typeface VTKS Velhos Tempos
Body text Garamond 12pt

Published by Blue Poppy Publishing, Devon

ISBN: 978-1-911438-85-4

To
Martin, Ruth and Anna.

CHAPTER 1

For the last thirty-five years I have kept a secret. Not some insignificant furtive little indiscretion, but a secret of such enormity that it would change the history books. Despite the magnitude of it, now and then when I cast my mind back to the decision I made at that moment I can't help but smile a little. It was a mischievous thing to do, but the deed was done in a split second, and anyway, I was just a child; how could I be to blame? The young are completely innocent of any consequences of their actions, so no, I don't carry any guilt. For ten years now I had created my own private pilgrimage to London just to view it, deriving such delight from the visit, I even made it my annual birthday treat. I could just sit all day and watch the people come and go to look at it whilst knowing that not one of them knew the truth.

Today is my birthday and I had my ritual all planned out except one small detail for which I was feeling a little apprehensive: my daughter, Maisie, had insisted on coming with me. Don't get me wrong, I love spending time with Maisie and on any other day would have been delighted to see her. But this annual trip was mine. I had never shared it. How could anyone get the same feeling as me without knowing the truth?

'Happy Birthday, Cat!" Maisie shouted as she let herself in my front door.

My full name was Catherine, which most people shortened to Cathy but Cat, which my dad always called me, was reserved for a few special people. I never liked to be known as 'Mum' either: I had always called my parents by their Christian names so it didn't seem unusual for me to continue this tradition with my own daughter.

"I'm looking forward to seeing what it is you find so fascinating that you need to visit every year." Although I had always gone to London alone, it wasn't a secret where I was going. Everyone knew I went to The National Gallery; they just didn't know why.

Maisie thrust a card in my hand saying, "I've ordered your present but it didn't arrive in time; sorry!"

There was no gift on order. It didn't matter; I knew she cared. Maisie was twenty-five now and living almost self-sufficiently in a flat with her latest boyfriend. Her mind was and always will be a complete whirlwind. She has never operated like most people. She sees the world in her own unique way: thoughts and questions pop up and down before leaving unanswered and her mind flitting onto another topic altogether.

"Thanks, great card. We'd better get going if we want to catch the early train."

We made our way to the station and caught the train to Waterloo. As we neared London, Maisie probed, "So come on then, what is so important in the art gallery that you come every year to see?"

"You'll see soon enough. How's Ben?" I said, diverting the topic.

"He's fine. Working in the hotel today. They offered him a few extra shifts, so we should be all right for money next month."

I knew that, despite her best efforts to be independent, life was tough. Money was tight, and she constantly felt she was missing out on some great adventure. Like so many others, despite having achieved a degree, the only work she could find was temporary bar work or some boring marketing telesales job. Left with a student debt and with the cost of living being so high I often wondered how things would ever get better for her.

The train pulled in to Waterloo station. Everyone began rustling about gathering their possessions ready to disembark and rush off to their respective appointments. We joined them. Although we were in no rush, it felt like we should merge in.

"We can walk to the gallery from here, just over the bridge and up to Trafalgar Square. Where do you fancy going for lunch later?"

"I don't mind, although I have been craving a decent halloumi burger."

We set off on the familiar walk from the station, heading for the London Eye before ambling along the river, up the steps and over the Jubilee Bridge to the Embankment. The sun was shining and despite a sharp wind, it was pleasant enough out. We headed straight up Villiers Street to Trafalgar Square. It seemed like every other unit had become a café now and I marvelled how everyone had so much time to sit around drinking coffee all day.

As soon as the steps of the gallery were in my sight I picked up the pace and once inside, I led the way straight across the Ground Floor Gallery, walking through the first two rooms before making a right turn and circumventing around another room and entering a larger space at the back titled 'Paintings after 1600'. Maisie followed behind, trying to avoid bumping into anyone as I sped through the galleries. My step began to slow as I concentrated my gaze on the usual spot. It was always so easy to see amongst the other large garish paintings; the one and only small black painting reflecting so much light from the side that you could hardly see it until you were directly in front. But today it wasn't there. I came to a complete stop right where it should have been. I stepped back and looked up and down the wall in complete disbelief. All of Goya's other paintings were there in their correct positions – 'The Duke of Wellington', 'Doña Isabel de Porcel', 'Don Andrés del Peral' and 'A Picnic' – but the painting I had come to see – 'The Forcibly Bewitched' was missing.

Maisie caught up and noticed my bewilderment. "What's up?"

"It's…it's not here."

"What's not here?" Maisie asked.

"The Forcibly Bewitched. That's so strange. It's been here in this position for years. Why would they move it?" I began pacing up and down the same stretch of wall again, manically searching for the painting. "Where is it?" I exclaimed. My voice was becoming too loud for the quiet gallery, and one of the stewards had noticed my apparent upset and began striding towards us, his moment of power finally arisen.

"Is everything all right here, ladies?"

"My mother has noticed the display is different to normal," Maisie tried to explain. Although I had calmed down enough to realise that I mustn't make any more of a scene, I still desperately needed to know where the painting was. I blabbered out quickly,

"Where is 'The Forcibly Bewitched' by Francisco de Goya, painted in 1798? It's always here, you know, the dark, mysterious painting with Don Camillo refuelling the oil lamp and dancing donkeys on the wall behind."

"Yes, I know the painting you mean," the steward countered impatiently. "The National Gallery recently procured a new, premium X-ray fluorescence machine, and seeing as you appear to know a lot about that particular painting, perhaps you will recall the story around its arrival here?" Before waiting for my answer he continued, "Therefore, it is of no surprise that it is one of the first paintings to undergo a thorough investigation with this state-of-the art piece of equipment."

I just stood there dumbfounded. I felt faint and sick at the same time. "Thank you," said Maisie. "I'll take it from here." With a look of concern she took my arm and led me over to the benches, so I could sit down. Once we were distanced from the steward and he seemed to accept the action was over, he returned to his post, although he continued to keep a sharp eye on us. "What is it, Cat?" Maisie whispered urgently.

I looked at her. I could feel my eyes begin to fill with tears. I knew that my hand would be forced and the truth would come out. It always does eventually. A lie is like ivy. At first when it starts to grow it looks pretty as it gently entwines itself across the wall, weaving and spreading. You leave it to develop thinking *what harm can it do?* Then before you know it, the stems have become thick with little claws that prevent them being moved or cut back. It becomes impossible to untangle as it grows thicker and stronger until it covers everywhere and there is nothing of the original wall left to see. Eventually it has to be poisoned to prevent further damage, often killing everything around it at the same time.

"It's a long story. Not here. Let's go find that halloumi burger."

We walked down to the South Bank and found a large innocuous chain restaurant where we could sit all day without interruption. Maisie ordered her burger and the latest power smoothie; I opted for a panini and orange juice. We sat quietly for a while, Maisie looking concerned, but knowing I would talk when I was ready. The drinks arrived and I took a deep breath.

"Every decision we make in our lives influences our future so it's important that I start from the beginning so you can understand my history and what happened during my childhood."

I began to tell Maisie the story of where I grew up, recollecting details that I hadn't thought about for years.

My childhood residence was in one of the most prestigious areas of Surrey, in a house surrounded by huge trees backing onto a golf course – not that anyone in the family played the game; we were just there for its status. The house had the grand name of High Trees and was on South Drive, with a main entrance that had stone pillars either side and wrought iron gates which were permanently wedged open. The driveway had a large circular flower bed in the middle which operated like a roundabout and in the centre of it there was what looked like a Christmas tree that had been allowed to grow to an enormous height.

High Trees had been built around 1950 and had a large kitchen, lounge, dining room and six bedrooms divided into three sections. There was also a conservatory and a large flat roof extension with a games room and indoor swimming pool. Despite the impressiveness of this residence and its celebrity location it was actually quite bland looking. The brick was a dull stone colour and the metal windows had been painted green many years previously. There was a substantial paved porch which led to the front door with a stone seat around two of the sides; a small window allowed the area to be viewed from inside the house. I remember that it was always cold. Only occasionally around Christmas would we have an open fire that would warm the place up temporarily.

Inside, the décor was a complete mismatch of styles and eras. In the hall there was an enormous shiny leather-topped antique table bigger than a king-size bed, then next to it a foldable table tennis table. There were grandfather clocks that chimed randomly next to battery-operated clocks whose hands ticked on the same spot over and over waiting to be reinstated. Ornaments that had been handed down for generations, some porcelain with delicate flowers painted on them, adorned the window sills; randomly in the corner, an almost life-size and very kitsch, glazed porcelain tiger. To complete the overall look was a very intense, abstract sixties patterned maroon carpet and wallpaper that had a risen pattern in gold felt. The rest of the house was similar with random miscellanea littered everywhere. Very occasionally a room would be redecorated but when all the items were put back it just continued to look like a fusion of the ages.

We moved there when I was five. I have no recollection of our previous home and it was never talked about. My parents had only just got married. They had met in 1969 when my mother, Ava, had just started her first secretarial job. She had been brought up in a tiny two-bedroom terraced house in Chiswick with her sister. Her parents had both had to endure hard-working manual jobs to provide enough food for the table, and she had already decided that wasn't going to be her future. She discovered she had a flair for English so it was the natural path for her to take a secretarial course.

Her very first post was in a motorcycle sales showroom called Fox Motors. All the salesmen flirted with her hoping for a quick fumble in the mechanics' area, but she coyly avoided their advances. The boss, Bob Fox, often had meetings with sales reps and other dealers and one sunny afternoon Bill, a tall, handsome man in a soft grey suit, walked through the showroom door for one such encounter. Bill was thirteen years older than Ava and was already married with two children, but on seeing Ava he was completely infatuated and quite simply fell madly and deeply in love.

Bill had been unhappy in his marriage for many years and this hint at a different life was all he needed to push him into a decision. He was a wealthy man who commanded incredible respect whenever he entered a room, gained after building up Riverdale Cars Ltd, a highly successful motor car business, over many years. Fortunately, Ava was just as captivated with Bill and after their first meeting knew just what she wanted. No one in Fox Motors had a bad word to say about Bill, and Ava was too young and smitten to worry about the potential consequences of breaking up a marriage. It took just two further meetings before they had started their affair.

It was to last for nine years during which they had two children, my brother Shawn and me, and throughout this time Bill had a bitter battle to divorce his first wife. High Trees was their new start; however, it came with new conditions.

During the divorce, Bill had provided numerous witnesses to substantiate the inability of his former wife to be able to care for their two children, Billie-Joe and Jane. Not only did he win sole custody of the children but also managed to have his ex-wife sent back to Germany, her home country. The two children were the condition for this new start with Ava; she was to take them on and bring them up alongside Shawn and me.

I haven't had any contact with my stepbrother and stepsister for years and I never really thought of them as my family anyway; I think Ava saw to that. She secretly chose High Trees as the six bedrooms were divided into three sections: at one end she put Shawn and me, in the middle herself and Bill and then right at the other end and as far away from her children as possible, Billie-Joe and Jane.

Sadly, family life was not as blissful as it should have been. To describe Ava's position as difficult is an understatement. Billie-Joe was fifteen when they moved in and Jane just thirteen. Understandably they did not take to their new 'situation' and loss of their mother very well. Billie-Joe adapted more quickly to accepting Ava; she was only fifteen years older than him, and they became quite close. He was, however, deeply emotionally scarred by what had happened during his childhood and soon turned to petty crime to vent his anger.

Jane took the rejection of her own mother and 'intrusion' of Ava particularly badly and would kick out at every opportunity. There were bitter battles between them, but Jane was a daddy's girl and was always careful to note if he was within earshot before lashing out a torrent of abuse. This made Ava look foolish if she ever complained, and not wanting to give the appearance that she couldn't handle a child, opted to put up and shut up, for a while anyway.

Being the youngest I quite enjoyed watching my older siblings and their antics. Billie-Joe used to play with Shawn in the garden sometimes: he would swing him round by his arms and I would be on the sidelines cheering him to go faster. One time he lost grip and Shawn went flying through the air and landed in the rose bed, dislocating his shoulder. Ava arrived on the scene demanding to know what had happened, but too many cries were coming from Shawn to get any sense from him as he sat on the ground covered in thorns with his arm clutched to his chest, and

Billie-Joe had long since legged it out of sight. I didn't say a word and as usual was soon left to my own devices as Ava whisked Shawn off to the hospital.

The garden went right around all sides of the house covering over six acres in total. There were many parts to it: a vegetable garden, a small field, some woods with an enormous monkey puzzle tree right in the middle, and an old mossy tennis court. It went on and on. At the very bottom of the field there was a huge hole in the ground that had been an outside swimming pool in the distant past and was now used to dump all the garden waste. There was nearly always a fire going in it or an area smouldering that I could poke and watch the red glow deep underneath the surface. Just beyond was a gate that led out onto the road wide enough to drive through.

All these grounds were cared for by just one gardener, an Italian man called Tony with skin that looked like worn leather. He had a slight limp when he walked, and he was very slow. He didn't speak English or even seem to understand it. Bill would give him instructions to cut the hedges, and he would go and cut the grass. You couldn't have a conversation with him; he would stumble around trying to find the words, making long indistinguishable noises in his thick Italian accent. I used to quite like teasing him by speaking really fast as if relaying an instruction, then running away. He had a tiny white pickup truck that I named Polly to drive around the garden and collect all the waste in. There was some kind of loyalty bond between him and Bill, and Tony stayed working in our garden for fifteen years.

Despite Ava's best efforts to try to coax me to have an interest in girly things I was a tomboy through and through. I wanted to be outside making mud pies and climbing in the trees, not cutting patterns out of flowery material for dressmaking. She had told me that from the time I could walk I was heading in my own direction – and that was the opposite one to hers. She had been best friends with her own mother and now, amidst all the family troubles she was having to endure, wanted to cultivate a friend more than ever, but I wasn't up for that position, and the harder she tried to mould me the further away she pushed me.

I wasn't like Jane though – mean and full of hatred. I could see how much she hurt Ava and I didn't want to add to that. I was simply distant, away in my own make-believe land, playing outside for hours in the secret passages around the garden, spying on the neighbours, sneaking into their gardens with a makeshift catapult of a twig and a rubber band to shoot conkers at them and make them jump. I knew my way around the garden and house so well and had created numerous dens and hiding holes. No one could ever find me. In desperation, Ava bought a big old brass bell and would stand outside and ring it, so I knew that meant it was time to go in – or else.

I have a strong memory of Billie-Joe coming into my room at night and climbing out the window onto the flat roof. He obviously chose my room as it was easy to climb in and out undetected. I was usually too sleepy to notice but if he came back when it was nearly light I sometimes noticed his face had blood on it and his hands were bruised. It frightened me but I just curled further under the blankets pretending to be asleep. I never asked where he had been. He would creep back up the corridor, to his end of the house, slip into bed and not appear until after everyone else had gone out for the day. He missed most of the final year of school and was then either out with his mates, sometimes for several days, or sleeping in his room.

Jane, however, became more difficult and troublesome in the home. She discovered the best way to get at Ava was to hurt Shawn. On several occasions she would take him off down the garden, coaxing him into playing hide-and-seek then forcing him to climb the highest tree until he got stuck or mixing up a concoction of crushed leaves and flowers and making him take a sip resulting in him being sick.

Ava pleaded with Bill over the severity of the situation until eventually after Jane's antics progressed to a rather more serious incident involving a kitchen knife, Bill had to admit the truth about his beloved Jane and at the age of fifteen she was sent to boarding school and back to her own mother in Germany.

Just below the driveway, there was an old hollow tree where I created a special hiding hole. In fact, I created dens and secret viewing spots everywhere. People would come and go all the time and I loved to spy on them.

A regular visitor was a well-built young man called Digger. He was friends with Billie-Joe, although he seemed older. He would just walk in the house at all sorts of odd times, stinking of cheap aftershave and beer. He looked untidy in his T-shirt and tight jeans, never wearing a suit like most of Bill's associates, yet was always offered hospitality. Ava would drop everything to offer him food or drinks, after which he would go down to the study with Bill who would close the door behind them.

I longed to know what they discussed in the study. I wasn't allowed in there but when no one was looking I sneaked in for a look around. It was in one of the extended parts of the house. It had windows on two sides and just outside the door was another door that led out into the garden. One of the walls had deep floor to ceiling cupboards, the ground level of which had sliding doors. Inside were numerous box files that looked like they hadn't been touched for years. I moved them around to create an inner hole that I could crawl into, leaving a gap so that I could reach out and slide the cupboard door closed behind me. Next time Digger turned up I would be ready.

Bill was out at work six days a week, selling cars and arranging repairs and MOTs for the mechanics to carry out. He left when we were having breakfast and came back just in time for dinner. Sometimes on a Saturday if I promised to keep out of the way I was allowed to go with him. I could easily keep myself occupied there. In the car park at the back of the repair centre there were several old sheds full of used promotional material: life-size cardboard cut-outs of 'happy families' that had once been placed next to the latest model, boxes full of balloons with 'free servicing for a year' written on them, pens, pencils and notepads with the garage address embossed in gold and old leather diaries years past their date. I could help myself to anything out there, and I often did, stuffing my pockets with stationery I could give away at school.

The repairs centre had a manager called Bernie. Numerous mechanics came and went over the years but Bernie was always there. He reminded me of Danny DeVito and always seemed very uneasy at me hanging around. He had a filthy little office in the corner of the garage and everything in it was covered in grease with files all smothered with dirty fingerprints and metal filing cabinets with papers hanging out. On the wall was a calendar with topless women which he tried to cover over if he ever saw me coming. Of course I had no interest in looking at that but what I really wanted was just outside his office and was the best thing of all – a hot drinks vending machine. For twenty pence I could get myself an instant hot chocolate, a treat that I would never be allowed at home. Bernie was always ready to provide me with the required money and would send me back to the showroom and away from him with my little plastic cup of sickly sweet liquid.

The offices were divided by thin walls with glass on the upper half so you could see inside them and right through to the showroom, and the floor was covered in cheap carpet tiles that were prickly. Bill's office had an enormous wooden desk and leather chairs. I liked to hide underneath in the footwell with my hot chocolate so no one could see me. There was a crack in the wooden panel on the front of the desk and I could just about see through to the doorway. Behind the door, in the corner there was a very old black dog; a mix of Rottweiler and boxer, it belonged to Bernie but liked to spend the day curled up in Bill's office. I didn't like it. It smelt old and it grumbled as it slept, but it didn't give me away, so we had a silent pact to leave each other alone. Numerous people would come and go throughout the day: customers, dealers, friends, but there was one thing they all had in common: they always talked about money.

I finished reminiscing momentarily as our food had arrived. After digesting her first mouthful of burger Maisie asked, "I never knew all this about you, Cat. You've never really spoken about your childhood; it's fascinating and I'd like to know more, but what has all this got to do with our experience in the gallery this morning?"

I paused a moment, deciding how best to continue. I could see Maisie wanted to understand why the missing painting was so important and what that had to do with my childhood, but now I had started recollecting other events, I felt there was so much more I wanted to tell her.

"Okay, let me skip forward to the end of the eighties, when I was about thirteen. Perhaps telling you the story of my childhood will also help me begin to acknowledge how my actions led to such dramatic consequences."

CHAPTER 2

The school summer holidays were endlessly dragging on, and one day I was so bored I decided to go to work with Bill. I was hiding under his desk colouring in an old diary when I heard voices approaching the office. Bill entered and perched on the edge of his desk. I could see his legs through the crack, and I was just thinking I ought to let them know I was there but as they were deep in conversation I opted to listen; I often found it fun to listen in on Bill's business deals. I recognised the voice; it was Ed who had been friends with Bill for some years. He was an amateur artist, and Bill had a few of his paintings dotted throughout the house that he'd acquired over the years.

"Come on, Bill, it's just a small advance, a drop in the ocean for you and I'll be able to pay it back in full plus interest within the year."

"What do you need it for?" Bill asked.

"Well you don't know my good friend and art tutor Nicholas, but in my opinion he is the leading expert at being able to replicate historical paintings. Honestly, I have never known anyone to be so incredibly talented. Although it's not common knowledge, I am certain he is behind some of the most famous forgeries painted in the last decade. Now, I have been thinking about this for a long time, and there is a window of opportunity coming up soon that I simply can't afford to miss. An art collection is being moved to The National Gallery, and Nicholas has a particular interest in one of the paintings. He has been studying the Old Masters' painting techniques for years, and I am confident he will be able to replicate one of the particular pieces they are moving in a very short amount of time."

"You're not planning to acquire it for him?" Bill asked in disbelief.

"I have meticulously planned this, Bill; all I need now is the capital for the incidentals. I already have a buyer in mind for the original, so I'll be able to pay you back quickly."

"Well, Ed, you know I've had my doubts about your plans before, but to your credit, you have always managed to prove me wrong. This time, however, I'm just not convinced you can pull it off. It's highly unlikely you can steal from an art gallery and get away with it."

"Ah BUT what if I did? This heist would go down in history! Come on, Bill, I know you like a gamble. I'll double your money then, how about that? I'll keep your name completely sacred – no one will ever know you backed me."

"If you don't I'll have you working for me free for the next five years! Let's flip this coin: heads you get your loan, tails you go elsewhere." I heard the coin turning through the air then slap down on the desk above my head.

"Ha! Okay, come back on Monday at noon," Bill told Ed. I heard a voice from across the showroom calling Bill. There was a customer waiting to see him. The men said their goodbyes and left the office.

I stayed in my little hiding hole for some time after they had gone thinking about what I had heard. An art robbery! It sounded like something from an American movie. Of course, I had no idea how serious Ed was and Bill seemed amused at the notion, as if anyone could really steal a painting. The whole idea was ridiculous.

At the end of the day, Bill counted the money that had come in, writing down the amounts in a little leather notebook he kept in his pocket, and putting the cash in an old worn plastic bag ready to take home and put in the safe. Once we were home, I kept close by. I loved to be around when the safe was opened; it held all sorts of treasures, and if there was time sometimes I was allowed a look.

First there was a very heavy metal door in the wall which had a funny key. This opened into a tiny cupboard-size room with just enough space to stand up. There were shelves around all the sides and on the ground a huge safe. This required another key that had to be screwed together. Bill kept half on his key ring and the other half was hidden under an old pile of papers. Once inside there were lots of boring packets and heaps of cash, old boxes with medals and watches, but at the very back on a little shelf was my favourite item – a gold charm bracelet belonging to Ava. Each of the charms did something, from a tiny book which actually opened to a harmonica that made a little noise. Bill passed it to me while he tinkered about inside the safe. I wanted to handle it for longer but a shrill voice sounded from the kitchen – Dinner's ready!

I passed the bracelet back. "Just pop and get me a couple of Distalgesics before dinner," he instructed me as he locked the safe.

Just after we all moved to High Trees, Bill had been diagnosed with multiple sclerosis. He had suffered with pain in his legs and after numerous X-rays and tests, his doctor who was also his best friend, Patrick, had come to the conclusion it was MS. He was prescribed medication and pretty much left to get on with it. If he asked me to fetch him a couple of Distalgesics along with his regular pills, I knew he was particularly suffering.

I went to the 'cat room', a sort of large lobby area where the cat slept. The walls were lined with old kitchen units, the kind you would have seen when fitted kitchens first became a thing. Packets of pills were kept high up in the corner one where the only way to reach them was to open the cupboard first then climb up onto the worktop balancing on the slippery top on my knees. The shelves were piled up with boxes and packets full of pills; tiny white ones and large flat ones. In the front there was the bottle for regular use; I knew to get two of the tiny white ones. Then behind in the packet were the Distalgesics. After popping a couple out I jumped down and carried the four pills to the kitchen.

Dinner was on the table. There were just the four of us eating tonight; Billie-Joe was out again.

In each of the place settings sat a plate of raw beetroot and apple salad with sultanas and honey dressing served as a starter. Ava was at the very beginning of what was to become a lifelong obsession with food, the first stage being that every meal must be started with some kind of raw vegetable.

I hated it and Shawn, sitting opposite me, also hated it. Even Bill occasionally refused to eat it and would have half an avocado or suchlike in his place instead of the weird coloured offering everyone else had to endure. Of course no one would dare mention it; we just simply sat in silence munching slowly until it was all gone before commencing the main dinner which was seldom much better. On this occasion it was a kind of bake: underneath a crispy top made of crushed cornflakes, cheese and whole wheat breadcrumbs were prawns and carrots swimming in a sauce that had become congealed where it hit the topping. The paste formed a skin as it cooled and I attempted to scrape it off and spread it over the surface of the plate hoping no one would notice I hadn't eaten it. Of course Shawn, an all-round mummy's boy, spotted my trick. He caught my eye and had a look of pure delight as he was just about to drop me right in it when the doorbell rang. I was saved.

"I've finished, so I'll get it," I said politely as I quickly jumped up, rinsed my plate in the sink and ran out of the kitchen, sticking my tongue out at Shawn and whizzing through the cat room and into the hall. The front door was never locked during the day; it was a large heavy dark wooden door with a bell at the top like the ones you see on shop doors to warn of impending customers. I pulled it open to reveal two policemen. One stood slightly behind with his hat still on, facing the other direction with a look of boredom, while the tall one in front asked me if Billie-Joe was home.

"I haven't seen him today," I lied and with a sigh the one in front simply said thanks and turned to leave.

Police knocking and looking for Billie-Joe was quite a common occurrence but whether he was in or not and whoever answered the door they would always get the same response. We all knew he had been up to no good – usually something to do with cars or stealing; just petty stuff.

I was closing the door again when another car pulled in the drive. It was Fat Jack, the accountant. Ava created nicknames for lots of Bill's acquaintances, very basically based around what they looked like or did, although it was a secret between her, Shawn and me. There was 'Fat Jack' of course, 'Trucker', a friend of Digger's, 'The Walker', a random tramp we used to see everywhere when we drove out of the estate, 'Prickly Pete', a thin-lipped man Bill would go to the auctions with, and then Ava's worst enemy, her mother-in-law, 'The Chatter Nan'.

Fat Jack was at the door now. "Well hello, young lady!" he said to me in his slimy posh schoolboy voice. He made my skin crawl. His lips were always wet and saliva would spit out when he spoke. He tried to make a lunge towards me but I saw it coming and managed to skip out the way saying, "Dad's in the kitchen."

I waited for him to go ahead then followed.

"Hello, Ava!" he bellowed as he entered the room. She wasn't as quick as me and had to endure a great wet kiss on the cheek. "Bill, good to see you."

"Jack, what can I get you to drink?" Ava asked him, also wanting to escape I could tell.

"Whisky, my lovely, if you please – no water."

Ava ducked out the kitchen, through the hall and down to a little walk-in cupboard by the garage where the ingredients were kept for every kind of drink anyone could possibly ask for. It was like a mini bar except some bottles at the back had been there so long they had got crystals around the caps, and the top shelf of glasses had a thick layer of dust on them. Bill mostly drank beer and there were plenty of those in stock. Ava liked Bacardi and Coke and sometimes a Tia Maria. I wasn't old enough to drink but very occasionally during the year would be allowed a Snowball – advocaat and lemonade with a glacé cherry on a stick in it. Once a month on a Sunday morning Bill would go down to the off-licence to replenish the supplies and if I went with him, he would also buy me a Bitter Lemon.

Ava found the whisky and poured a generous serving into one of the crystal glasses that had come free from the garage, picked up a bottle of beer for Bill and headed back. Bill and Fat Jack had moved to the lounge now and were just lighting cigars. Ava handed each of them their drinks, and as she turned to leave got a little smack on her bottom off Jack as he laughed, "A little more generous with the whisky next time, my lovely." But she just carried on out the room with no comment while I slipped behind the back of the sofa unnoticed.

"So Bill, I need to get straight down to business tonight; Sal's waiting for me to get home for my dinner. To put it bluntly, you need to 'redistribute' some takings.

I've got an idea which will sort you out; I can make all the arrangements, nothing for you to do…except cough up the cash!" Jack took a big gulp of his whisky before carrying on. "You need to open a fictitious company; let's call it ABC Cars for example – Ava Bill Children – get it? You can pop the cash into a non-existent building – don't panic, my son Charles can sort that for you, and that can be your 'premises' for the new company. Sorts out that spare dosh and keeps you out of trouble! We can register the new company here to your home address and I can send the cash overseas for re-investment. We can put anything else 'spare' you make in the next year or two into the new company which after say five years we can make insolvent and blah, blah, blah…nice little nest egg for you when you are grey! What do you say?"

"Sounds good, Jack. I trust you not to leave any trail; with Billie-Joe's behaviour of late, I need to appear nice and clean."

"Well of course, what do you take me for? I'm used to dealing with such…shall we say, individual finances. It's all very complicated, Bill, but I don't want to bore you with all that. Anyway, the less you know the better…however, I would need to work around the clock to get it set up…means a few more hours…and of course it is my neck on the line…shall we say an annual fee of ten per cent?"

"Eight per cent, Jack." Bill stood up to shake hands.

Jack downed his last drop of whisky, struggled out of his chair and gave Bill a big slap on his back saying, "Very well, old friend, as it's you. Oh, just one more thing. In order to sort the 'property' and avoid the tax man, all monies need to come to me in cash – get that pretty little secretary of yours to run it over to my office first thing."

As they said their goodbyes on the porch I snuck upstairs to my room as if I had been there the whole time.

That Saturday was the first of the month which meant there was an auction. Bill often took the afternoon off work in order to go. He brought home the odd thing but really he was there to do business of his own. Occasionally I went along, but it was a bit boring. However, this Saturday it had been raining non-stop and I had been watching TV all morning, and was facing the prospect of an afternoon of card games with Shawn and Ava, so when Bill came home from work early in order to go, I decided to tag along too.

It was in an old Victorian barn round the back of town. Large double doors led from a courtyard into the auction room, and due to the rain everyone was packed inside. There was a low rumbling sound of talking and the air was thick with smoke. Everyone there seemed to know Bill, and they all tried to have a quick word with him. I left Bill talking to a couple of men in suits I didn't recognise and weaved through the hordes of legs to have a look around at this month's old offerings.

Furniture was precariously piled high, some nearly up to the ceiling; mostly dark, heavy wooden chairs and tables, the odd wardrobe and bed frame. Dusty bookcases lined a whole wall interspersed with cardboard boxes stuffed with antique books. Near the front there were glass-topped cabinets full of jewellery. Zigzagging along the aisles it was all the same boring stuff, then I saw it: a carved wooden elephant, it was distressed-looking as coloured paint had worn away over the years. It was fairly big, about the size of a large dog, and I really wanted it. I looked around to get Bill's attention. I saw him, but he was with one of his good friends, Richard, so as I knew he would be a while decided to go over to him.

When I reached them, Richard was talking about a party he was having next Saturday. He winked at me. I liked Richard; he was not like all the other dull friends Bill had. He was a bit younger than them to start with, wore bright coloured clothes, had a black stubbly beard, and always looked like he was smiling. He worked independently for several of the car dealers as a courier delivering the very expensive sports cars. Everyone trusted him, and he was great with the top-end customers. On delivery, he would have to demonstrate all the new gadgets to the customer and take them out for a trial run. He might have made a good parent but despite being married to April for many years didn't have any children of his own. I'd overheard Ava gossiping about them having IVF without success.

As I hovered beside them he said to me, "Will you come to our party and be a waitress? April really needs someone to hand round the nibbles. I know she'll get you a special present if you agree to help."

"Yes!" I replied. How cool to get to go to one of the adult parties instead of being stuck with the babysitter as usual.

Bill looked less pleased but didn't say I couldn't go. I thought it best to leave while the going was good and not to push my luck with the elephant.

CHAPTER 3

"Hey, little sneak." Billie-Joe made me jump. I was poking the smouldering bonfire and my thoughts were miles away.

"I want you to do something for me when you go to Richard's party Saturday."

"I'm going to waitress," I replied in my high and mighty voice.

"It won't take you a minute; everyone will be drunk by nine and they won't notice if you slip off. Just creep into Richard's study and look for the delivery schedule from 'Fox Motors'. Richard is going to deliver a Bugatti and I need to know the date, time and delivery address."

"As if! What if I get caught?"

"Look, if you don't do it I'm going to uncover all your little hidey holes – don't think I haven't seen you sneaking around spying on everyone, and while you are at school I'll have a good look round your bedroom and see what other secrets you are hiding. Anyway, you won't get caught; you're a pro."

"Fine," I agreed. I didn't want my secret places to be discovered. I was already going to have to think of some new ones, and I certainly didn't want anyone rooting around my room. I have to admit I was also a little flattered to be thought of as a professional spy.

When Saturday came I was dressed in my smart black trousers and white shirt just like a proper waitress. I was excitedly waiting for Bill and Ava in the hall, anxious to get to the party. I had a little bag with me with my notebook in it and a jumper in case I was cold, as well as my Walkman for the journey.

Shawn had been allowed to have a friend round for a sleepover and together they were being so annoying. He was old enough not to need a babysitter, although Ava felt better that he wasn't completely alone in the house. At last, they came down the stairs; Bill looked the same as a work day – suit and tie but in a slightly lighter grey than usual and Ava was wearing a dress she had made herself. The material was a sort of metallic blue and silver which flared out below the waist and would no doubt make quite a statement on the dance floor. Her feet were crammed into heels that were so pointed I wondered how on earth she could walk.

Finally, we left – leaving Shawn and his friend with a video to watch and a large bowl of home-made popcorn and squash Ava had left out as a treat. Richard and April's house was about a fifteen-minute drive away, so I settled in the back of the car with my headphones on. Ava checked me out of the corner of her eye in the mirror to see if I was listening to music. I nodded my head along and mouthed the words of a song, gazing out of the window and pretending to be oblivious to them in the front. She started talking quietly to Bill.

"How are your legs tonight? I know you struggle after a long day."

"Generally I seem to be packing up," Bill half joked. "More pain, so I take more pills but nothing actually makes it better. Patrick just says it will come and go like that, but I was talking to John about his symptoms, and they are not really all that similar. He has lots of other issues as well as the mobility like me and his definitely do come and go."

"John was diagnosed a long time before you…look, I know Patrick is your friend but do you think it would be worth getting a second opinion?"

"I'll have another chat with Patrick when he comes over next week. See if there are any different drugs I could try."

I worried about Bill's pain getting worse. I'd noticed he was walking slower, and he got cramp all the time now and made lots of heavy sighing noises, but he always tried to make light of it in front of me. He never ran around anymore either, and I was fetching his painkillers most evenings.

"Here we are," Ava mouthed at me. "You can unplug now."

Richard and April's house was not nearly as big as ours. It was a typical eighties semi-detached house on a road with numerous others all looking the same. Inside though it was unique. The rooms had funky wallpaper and the furniture was all rounded and bright. Music was already blaring out which you could hear from the drive although we were almost the first to arrive.

"Thank goodness you're here!" April called out from the doorway. "I was beginning to wonder if I was going to have to waitress myself all night." She gave me a little cuddle and ushered me into the kitchen, rapidly giving me instructions on what to do. "Take the coats upstairs to the study, hand round these cold plates first while you pop the others in the oven to warm. Don't worry about the drinks; Richard will sort those. If anyone wants a top-up just send them my way, and don't look so worried; it's a party, you can have some fun too!"

I was not worried about the job, it was what Billie-Joe wanted me to do that was making me feel sick. At least I would have a good excuse to go up to the study.

The guests started to arrive, and I took their coats and rushed upstairs to the study with them. Before I had a chance to look around more people arrived, and I was running up and down the stairs, then in the kitchen, then handing round the food, and before I knew it, it was nearly nine o'clock. Billie-Joe was right: everyone was quite drunk now. The nibbles were finished and the crowd was pouring out into the garden, the music getting louder and the guests getting rowdier. Now was my chance. I slipped upstairs and into the study.

I had piled all the coats on a small sofa and the office chair but avoided the desk. Quickly I scanned the papers on top, but there was nothing about Fox Motors. I tried to open the desk drawers; the small top drawer was locked and there was nothing relevant in any of the others, just old papers and invoices. I needed to find the key for the top drawer; I rummaged around under pen pots and books but there was nothing. I was thinking I had been gone quite a while and would have to give up, Billie-Joe would tell on me, and I would have to take the consequences, but as I made for the door I spotted Richard's bright blue jacket hanging on the back of it. I reached into the pockets and found a bundle of keys and took them back to the desk. I knew it would be the smallest one, and I was right. I slid open the drawer and there on the top was a diary.

Flicking through the next week's pages, I found an entry with the title '10am Fox Motors, Bugatti' and a name and address underneath. I quickly copied the details down in my notebook, placed the diary back in the drawer, locked it again and replaced the keys. I heard April calling my name in the distance. I didn't have time to get back downstairs, so I quickly slipped out of the study and into the bathroom, quietly locking the door behind me. Shortly afterwards there was a soft knocking on the door.

"It's April; are you OK?" She was quite drunk and was slurring her words. I opened the door and said I felt a bit sick. "Oh dear, I know what would help. Come with me." She took me into her bedroom and sat me down on the bed. "I bought you a little gift for helping out tonight." She fetched a tiny, perfectly wrapped box with a pink bow on the top off her dressing table and handed it to me. My cheeks started to burn. I was feeling guilty, my hands went all sweaty and I felt my eyes begin to fill with tears. April just thought I was shy and not feeling well so quickly diverted the attention. "Open it when you get home if you like. Come on, let's go downstairs and find your folks amongst all the rabble!"

Once in the car, Ava turned to me. I could see she was annoyed at having to leave the party early in order to take me home and said, "I think we will have to wait until you are a bit older before you can come to grown up things again. As soon as we get home it's straight to bed for you."

Fine by me, I thought; I was exhausted. Once alone and in bed I took out the little gift from April and slowly unwrapped it to reveal a delicate necklace with a tiny gold heart pendant. Although it wasn't something I would personally have chosen, I would treasure it forever.

The next day I was rudely woken by Billie-Joe crashing into my room. "So, what did you find out?" he gruffly asked.

I rubbed my eyes and sat up still half asleep. "Pass me my bag," I said and pointed to my rucksack on the floor.

He picked it up and threw it on my bed. I took out my notebook and found the page where I had written the address from Richard's diary. Billie-Joe grabbed it from my hand and studied the page. A wide smile appeared across his face before ripping it out and departing with the words, "Good one, sneak; I'll let you off this time."

I flopped back down in bed, relieved my hiding places were safe and promptly went back to sleep.

Later on, as it was Sunday afternoon, it meant alternate weeks of either visiting Bill's brother, Terry, and family or them visiting us. This week was our turn to go to them. It involved a drive into London followed by a long boring afternoon of sitting with the adults eating home-made cakes while they talked. Terry and Jean had four children, but they were all older than me – and didn't want me hanging around with them anyway. Shawn was just about old enough to tag along with them which meant I was usually left with the oldies.

This week though Terry had a new TV installed in the playroom and set it up so all the youngsters could watch a film, so I quietly sat on the floor with them hoping no one would notice me. My cousin Mark had acquired a copy of *Die Hard* which I knew had only recently come out at the cinema and was rated 15+, so I was trying to be particularly invisible.

After about half an hour Ava came in to see who wanted cake; it was right at the moment one of the hostages was shot. She spotted me and immediately instructed me to get out whilst telling the others they should know better than to let me watch such things.

"You can come and help me make the tea," she said in her soothing voice, as if that was going to help the disappointing situation. I was so annoyed; the movie was fine, and watching Bruce Willis strut around in a vest killing people wasn't going to scar me for life. I knew there was no point in arguing though and dutifully followed her to the kitchen, vowing silently to myself not to speak to her for the rest of the day.

Jean was already there setting out trays full of cakes she had been baking all morning. The second I walked in she gave me a job to do. "Go and get the small plates from the side cupboard and take them into the lounge." I collected the plates and carried them off to the men in the lounge. I was just at the door when I heard a new voice, so I sidled quietly into the room.

A man wearing leather biker gear, who I hadn't seen arrive, was talking. It was Dave; I had met him a few times, but he was mostly a friend of Terry's. He was a bit overweight, and looked ridiculous in the tight black leather. As I looked at him more closely I noticed his shirt was grubby, stubble was growing on his chin and his hair was greasy.

"Please, Bill. It won't be for long; I just don't have the space and Suzy is driving me mad with her moaning. The sales have been going well, and they want me to accept this big consignment – a shipping container full of supplies. I can shift them quickly…I'm under huge pressure to take them…actually I've already agreed…they have a way with words…if you know what I mean."

"If I agree to store them for you, Dave, I'm going to want some guarantees. You will have to put the container in my garden, round the back of the extension, so it can't be seen from the drive, but I don't want them knowing where I live, so make sure you are discrete. Then I'll need my own cut on the sales." There was a little chuckle from Terry – he'd heard many a deal made by Bill and found this amusing. "Finally, I'll want it all cleared up within six months."

Ava and Jean came in with the tea and cake just then and the men stopped talking. Typical, I thought, just as it was getting interesting. I guessed that by 'supplies' Dave must mean car and motorbike stuff. He had been in the trade just like most of the friends Bill had, except I recall him hitting a rough patch and losing his showroom. He must now just be selling spare parts. Anyway, the conversation shifted to the topic of holidays and I zoned out for the rest of the day.

CHAPTER 4

Finally, after what seemed like an eternity the new term started, although it didn't take long for me to remember how much I hated Secondary School. Most of the teachers didn't seem to like me and despite having a few friends I still couldn't wait to leave every day. The only lesson I could tolerate was art, and that was mostly due to thinking about Ed's plan, although there was also an interesting new art teacher who had started last term, Miss Avery, and at just twenty-two years old, this was her first post. She was tall and slim with brown hair so long it touched her waist. During her lessons we were allowed to listen to music and drink tea. She always seemed keen to chat to me and I would stay behind to talk to her sometimes, although I was careful not to divulge too much information about my home life. I began to quite enjoy the art lessons and with her encouragement discovered I was actually quite talented at drawing.

"How difficult is it to make a forgery?" I asked her one day.

"Oh well, it would take years of learning the techniques of the individual artist, then the new piece would need to be aged which is nearly impossible…oil paint smells for years while it dries out you see; old paintings wouldn't smell so it would be very difficult to replicate that. There are other simple things like the thread count of the canvas and whether staples were used or not – older pre-eighteenth century paintings wouldn't have had staples. Art dealers, museums, and galleries have many specialised staff that are experts in their field as well as various pieces of equipment to help them spot a fake. Why do you ask?"

"I was just thinking about trying," I joked, knowing this would throw her off the scent.

"It's much better to come up with your own masterpiece, don't you think?" she joked back.

I enjoyed Miss Avery's company, we really clicked, and in fact I think she was probably the only one who really *got* me.

The home bell went, and I said goodbye to Miss Avery thinking about how Nicholas was going to make the copy, assuming Ed managed the robbery at all.

When Ava picked me up she was anxious to tell me some news; the second I got in the car she started talking. "Richard has been injured and a Bugatti has been stolen!"

I wanted to process this information for a moment but Ava just carried on.

"You know how Richard does all the expensive sports car delivery jobs? Well my old boss, Bob, had him booked in to deliver a Bugatti this morning. On the way to the customer, when he was driving through the Blue Forest – you remember where we went for a picnic in the summer – he was stopped by a gang at gunpoint, and forced to get out of the car. He was then tied up while the gang stole the Bugatti! Poor Richard was stuck in the forest for hours until a dog walker found him and he could report what had happened. By that time the criminals had long gone!"

I was numb; I couldn't think what to say. Thoughts were racing through my mind. I had completely forgotten, but now I remembered today was the date I had copied down from Richard's diary. Ava looked over at my stunned face when we stopped at the traffic lights.

"I know, it's incredible. What a thing to happen!"

She thought I was simply surprised at her news, but that was far from what I was considering. I was thinking about Billie-Joe, and who he had told, and what if he had told someone it was me that had looked in Richard's diary, and what if they came looking for me with their guns? As the lights changed to green, Ava drove on and continued talking.

"Apparently Richard's been taken to the police station. I don't believe for a moment he's involved but Bob is already blaming him as the car was in his care, and no one else knew about this delivery. Richard is under very strict confidentiality agreements not to disclose this kind of information, and has to keep all relevant documents under lock and key. Of course, it's no secret that he and April have been struggling financially since the IVF treatment costs…and they have taken a second mortgage on the house. Do you know how much a Bugatti costs? Over a million pounds! No, I don't believe it. Oh, how frightening to be held at gunpoint!"

Ava babbled on until we got home, but I had stopped listening and was feeling desperate to talk to Billie-Joe.

Once in the house I went straight upstairs claiming I had homework to do, but after sitting on my bed for a few minutes trying to think of a rational reason yet being unable to, I stomped up the corridor to Billie-Joe's room.

His bedroom was usually locked but the door was ajar, so I went in. He wasn't there. In fact as I looked around the room I noticed not much of his stuff was there either. I opened the wardrobe; there were just a few empty hangers and some clothes screwed up in the bottom. It took me a moment to digest what was staring me in the face, and with slow horrifying revelation I knew what had happened. He was the gunman, and I was more than just an accomplice to this terrible crime; I was responsible.

For the next week all anyone spoke about was the Bugatti theft. Richard had been released from the police station without charge and was back home. The only fragment of information he had about his attackers was that the one that tied him up had an overpowering scent of Lynx, which of course didn't particularly help the police. All his future jobs had been cancelled. Bill had been over to visit him, but he simply had no idea how the theft had happened and was desperately traumatised. He was panicking how he was going to pay his debts without any work. His characteristic happy smile was gone, replaced with the look of worry and despair.

Over dinner that evening, out of the blue, Bill said to me, "When we were at Richard's party, and you were in charge of taking coats to the study, did you see anyone acting suspicious?"

I was caught by surprise and felt my cheeks start to burn and my eyes well up. A shake of my head was all I could manage.

Ava immediately started spouting potential scenarios again. "Did you see Brian at the party? I never liked him; I wonder if he has anything to do with this."

I could tell Bill wasn't listening to her though, and I could feel he was just looking at me.

I felt desperately sick about what I had done, but also a burning rage at Billie-Joe for making me do it. I had hardly said a word since realising what had happened, and with all the drama no one had noticed Billie-Joe had been absent for a whole week. I imagined him somewhere hot by now. He would have traded the car immediately and fled the country with the cash leaving me to face the consequences. How could he use me like that? As soon as dinner was over I made my excuses about having extra homework to do now I had started GCSEs, and went back up to my room.

I couldn't concentrate on homework though, and began going over it again and again in my mind. I was miles away in thought when I was suddenly aware of my door opening and Bill walking in. He never came up to our bedrooms unless it was serious. I can only recall him coming in once before, and that was when I had broken an ornament then attempted to hide it in the bin.

"Catherine, I know something's up," he said, standing in the middle of the room. "You will feel better once it's out in the open. What do you know?"

Bill never used my full name unless I was in trouble; I felt tears starting to fall, and I knew I was going to have to confess. There was no way of getting out of this now he had asked a direct question. My father wasn't someone you lied to. I spent a few moments trying to think of the right words and hoping Ava would call him downstairs for a phone call or something, anything just so he would stop staring at me. But there was just silence and that stare until I had no choice. I came clean.

I told him about Billie-Joe and the diary in between sobbing and denying I knew what was going to happen. He waited patiently for me to tell the whole story without moving or changing expression. Once I had finished, he stepped towards me and firmly took hold of my shoulders. He had a look I had never seen, a look of absolute fury, and despite my face and top now drenched in tears, he showed no sympathy but said with a voice quaking with anger, "Don't ever, ever talk about this to anyone ever again."

He gave me one last long look in the eyes as if to impose an unsaid bond between us, roughly released his grip on my shoulders and left the room.

After several minutes, overwhelmed with emotion, my anger with Billie-Joe returned. I was furious with him for tricking me, but it occurred to me that I was even more annoyed with myself for not spotting it first. I vowed not to let anyone fool me again.

As time went on, the rumours about the robbery began to fade. No one connected Billie-Joe's disappearance to it, and why would they? Ava wasn't bothered where he had gone; she was pleased to just have her own children around without worrying about Billie-Joe's influences. He was an adult now anyway and out of her control. Shawn was sixteen, and she didn't want him to start replicating the bad behaviour. She was surprised Bill didn't seem worried, but decided that they had probably just had a row and Billie-Joe was lying low for a bit.

One evening after dinner, Richard came over for a drink. It was about 8pm and Ava wanted to watch *Dynasty* on TV, so Bill took Richard down to the study. I had been spending as much time as possible alone in my bedroom, so no one questioned my absence. After a few minutes, I crept downstairs and along the corridor to the study door. If I got caught here there was nowhere to hide; the corridor was long and there were no other rooms to duck into. It was a big risk but I simply had to know what Bill was going to say. The study door was shut, so I had to go right up close to hear anything. Richard was talking; he sounded very different to his old buoyant self. His words ran together as he spoke like he hadn't slept in days and couldn't make his mouth work properly.

"It looks like they are going to repossess the house. April is inconsolable. We spent everything on the IVF last year and borrowed against the house for the third attempt, which didn't even work. No one will give me any work and my name and reputation are shot to bits. Sometimes I wonder what the point of even going on is."

Bill's response was swift. "Don't talk like that. You are my friend and I'm going to see that you and April get back on track. Starting with a loan of twenty thousand pounds."

There was a moment's silence before Richard stammered, "Bill…I…I…I can't think what to say. I can't take your money…no…I—" then the sound of a grown man crying, then, "I can't believe your kindness." There were more weeping noises, then, "But how can I ever pay you back?"

"I've been needing an extra pair of hands at the garage. Might as well be you as having to go through the bother of interviews. Come and work for me, take the money now so you and April can stay in your home, have one more go at IVF even, then start work full-time for me and I'll take a bit back from your wages each month as repayment. It won't be easy work though, and you'll have to stay in the showroom while all the talk blows over, which it will in time, Richard; you know what the gossips are like."

I'd heard enough and couldn't risk being discovered, so I soundlessly ran back up to my room to mull over what I had just heard. This was guilt money. Bill hadn't admitted that his children were responsible for Richard's near suicide, but was going to pay him back anyway. It was going to all be all right after all. I felt such relief, I could finally put it behind me and move on.

CHAPTER 5

"Have you seen what's in the garden?" Shawn asked me during a rare moment alone together in the kitchen after school.

"No, what?" I asked with my mouth full.

Ava was off on her new keep-fit frenzy with one of the neighbours, and Shawn and I were taking advantage of the situation by stuffing ourselves with biscuits; normally we would only be allowed one each.

"The massive shipping container! It's like the size of a lorry. It's hidden so you can't see it from the drive or any window in the house. I tried to open it to see what was inside, but it's bolted and there's a padlock," Shawn told me.

"That will be Dave's. They must have driven it up through the garden from the bottom gate," I told him casually like I knew it was there all the time. "I heard him asking to store some supplies here."

"What kind of supplies?" Shawn asked.

"I don't know, just motor parts I guess."

"Well I want to have a look. Where do you think the key is?" Shawn looked at me earnestly.

I didn't know where the key was, and I was cross I hadn't spotted the container before Shawn. I knew it was because I had been spending most of my time in my room this last week and hadn't ventured out into the garden for a while, but I was still annoyed. However, I did want to have a look inside, so I agreed to find the key. Bill was still at work, so now was a good time.

I instructed Shawn to keep a look-out for Ava returning, and started to have a look around all the usual places a key might be. There was nothing new on any of the key hooks, nothing in the study or lying on the tables. I thought perhaps Bill had put it on his key ring and taken it to work with him then one last spot came to mind. The garage key was kept on a hook above the back door. I reached up and there was another tiny key on the hook – a padlock key.

"Found it!" I said to Shawn with a shrewd grin on my face.

"Come on, let's go," Shawn said.

It was just beginning to get dark outside, and when we got to where the container stood I couldn't believe how big it was. An enormous great tank, slightly rusted, and with old green paint peeling off loomed above me. It was so peculiar just seeing this thing dumped in our garden. There were double doors on the end the same height as the container.

We undid the padlock but the bolt was really heavy, and we had to both lift and turn it together. Then we pulled the door slightly open, and what light there was left spilled inside. I could just about make out loads of different sized wooden crates stacked haphazardly. Shawn slipped in and tried to open one, but they were nailed shut. We were going to need a hammer to wrench one open. Just then, we heard a car on the drive; Ava was back, and would want to know where we were. Shawn was very nervous about getting caught, so we decided to push the door closed and not bolt the container, and just slip the padlock on unlocked, so we could come back later. We snuck back into the house, and Shawn kept Ava's attention while I planted the key back where I had found it.

We had to do our homework before dinner, but I couldn't concentrate. I'd seen plenty of spare parts in the mechanics' area at Bill's work and knew how they were usually packaged, and I'd never seen any in wooden crates. I knew we couldn't leave the padlock undone for long in case Bill noticed, so decided to investigate further that night.

After dinner, Bill remained at the table reading the paper while Shawn and I were washing up. Ava was on the phone to her sister. I whispered to Shawn to come to my room at midnight, so we could climb out my window to have another look in the container.

"Nah, I can't be bothered," he whispered back.

How could he give up so quickly? What a baby not wanting to go out at night. "Chicken! Well I'm going to go," I said defiantly.

I had a torch of my own, but I was going to need the hammer. It was kept in a tool box in the garage. I wasn't allowed to go in the garage, and with everyone around I was going to have to come up with a good excuse.

Ava came back in after her call; she looked worried. Her mother who lived with her sister down in Cornwall had had a fall and broken her wrist. Her sister was due to go on holiday, and now wouldn't be able to leave her mother alone, so needed Ava to go down and stay.

"When does she need you to go?" Bill asked.

"During half-term in a couple of weeks," replied Ava. "I can't really say no. She does look after her all the rest of the time. Why don't I take the kids? We can make it into a holiday!" She looked in Shawn's and my direction beaming expectantly.

"Who is going to make my dinner?" Bill said. Typical, I thought. I don't think I'd ever even seen him make himself a cup of tea.

I didn't particularly want to go anyway, so I said, "It's fine, I'll stay. I have a big school project to do anyway. Talking of which, Miss Avery has asked us to draw some tools for homework. Can I borrow a few from the garage?"

Bill got up. "I'll get you some," he said and made off in the direction of the garage, obviously keen for me not to discover the new key.

"She said to make sure I included a spanner, a screwdriver, oh and a hammer," I called after him.

Shawn looked with sheer disbelief at my cunning. Bill came back with a whole selection of tools for me, including the hammer.

"Thanks. I'll leave them by the back door tomorrow when I've finished," I said and I took the tools upstairs.

Later that evening, I had to wait until eleven-thirty before everyone had gone to bed. I watched for the corridor light to go out before getting out of bed and getting dressed. I opened my window; it was freezing outside. I'd seen Billie-Joe come and go often, so I knew there must be a good way down. I climbed onto the flat roof and peered over the edge, looking with my torch. There was a large branch of a tree almost touching the flat roof, so I clambered onto the branch and swung down to the ground. It wasn't easy, especially with my rucksack which had the hammer inside. Once down I looked back up, worrying if getting back was going to be so easy but decided to get on with what I had come to do for now.

It was eerie in the garden on my own at night, and creeping around in the dark. I heard leaves rustle and owls hoot, and I felt quite nervous. I reached the container and removed the padlock. I'd forgotten how heavy the door was; I put the torch on the ground, pointing towards the container, and with both hands I put all my strength behind the door, and with a sudden piercing rasp it swung open. I switched the torch off quickly and waited in silence, hoping no one heard the noise. After a few tense seconds, assuming the coast was clear, I put the torch back on and entered the void.

My hands were freezing now and felt a bit sticky. I shone the torch on them. I had cut myself somehow and they had blood on them. I don't know how it had happened; it must have been the tree or maybe the door, but they didn't hurt, probably because they were so cold, so I thought it best to just keep going. I crept inside and looked for a crate to open. Picking a small one I gently eased the end of the hammer under the lid. Once it was in, I started to move it backwards and forwards slowly levering the top off the crate. I had to do both ends before it popped open.

I hadn't actually thought about what would be inside other than that it wouldn't be motor parts, so I felt quite apprehensive now as I shone the torch inside. There was straw with metal showing underneath. I parted the straw and grabbed a piece of metal, holding it up in the torchlight. It wasn't a motor part – it was a gun!

I immediately dropped it back in the crate and stood up. I just looked at it there on the straw, not quite believing what I had discovered. I opened another crate – it was the same. The whole container must be full of them.

Amongst the straw and guns were little white boxes of bullets. Despite being alarmed, it wasn't the first time I had ever seen a gun. My Uncle Terry had several, including an air rifle, and he had taught me one Sunday how to hold them and load the pellets. These seemed much heavier, even though they were just small handguns.

I knew Shawn would never believe me and there must have been at least a hundred in the crates, so I took one gun and one box of bullets, and put them in my rucksack. I did it quickly, not giving myself time to think.

Then I began the impossible task of trying to nail the crates shut quietly. I put each nail back in its original hole and put my rucksack strap over the head to try and muffle the sound. The noise wasn't too loud, and I had no choice but to just get on quickly and put the crates back exactly as they were. I closed the door; again it squeaked, but I kept going and dropped the bolt back down, and sealed the padlock, praying the noise hadn't disturbed anyone in the house.

I made my way back to the tree, and scrambled up and onto the flat roof and back through the window and into the safety of my warm bedroom. I took a moment just standing still, listening out for any movement, but the house was silent, seemingly oblivious to my daring feat.

I had a sink in my room where I quietly washed my hands. I saw the wound which wasn't too bad, so I just wrapped some tissue around it, before sitting on the bed and gingerly taking out the gun from my rucksack.

I put it on my flowery duvet and spent ages just looking at it. Why was the container full of guns? Did Bill know what was in there? I looked at the box of bullets, removing several and fondling them, wondering how they would load inside the gun. I rested my finger on the pointed tip, then suddenly I became overwhelmed with a feeling of panic – what if Dave realised a gun was missing? Why did I take one? Should I put it back? How could I be so stupid?

I went to my chest of drawers and found an old T-shirt. Rapidly putting the bullets back inside their box, I wrapped the gun and white box of bullets in it, and stashed it underneath a pile of jumpers in my bottom drawer. It could stay there while I worked out what to do with it. I decided not to tell Shawn about it; there was no point in involving him now; he would panic and tell Bill.

I changed into my pyjamas and climbed into bed thinking I would never be able to sleep but immediately found myself in a deep slumber and didn't wake up until the alarm was ringing at seven. When Shawn asked me over breakfast what I had discovered I told him it had been spare parts, and was really boring, so I'd locked the container back up. He was easily satisfied, and I knew he would now leave the subject alone and move onto something else.

The Saturday of the half-term soon came around and Ava and Shawn were loading the car for their trip to Cornwall. It had been decided that I would go to work with Bill during the week. I had to sort the breakfast and make a packed lunch for us in the morning, and Ava had prepared several dinners which she had left in the freezer so all I had to do was heat them up in the evening. As we said our goodbyes I wondered if I had made the right choice to stay behind. Bill must have noticed my expression because as they drove off he said, "Sod the frozen meals; we'll get a Chinese takeaway for the first night shall we?"

Immediately I felt better; a Chinese takeaway would be a real treat. "We need to pop round to see Nan this morning, then Patrick is coming over this afternoon. You can do some homework then."

He had set the itinerary for the day. I knew whilst Patrick was there I would have to make myself scarce. I didn't want to go to see Bill's mother though. Ava called her the 'Chatter Nan' because she talked so much. Although she still lived alone, she was beginning to lose her wits, and would ask me to do strange things like stroke an invisible cat, or talk to the monkeys in the tree outside the front door. Anyway I knew it best to just agree, and I was still trying to keep a low profile after the Richard incident, although Bill acted like it had never happened.

The Chatter Nan's house was only a ten-minute drive. I got to sit in the passenger seat while Bill drove us there.

When we arrived he turned to me and said he knew it was a bit weird, but it was better to just agree to her unusual requests than make her think she was going mad. It wouldn't be long before she needed to go into a home and have proper care. Just keep her happy a little longer.

After the visit we went back home, had a quick sandwich and Bill went to his study telling me to send Patrick down to him when he arrived. I set up my homework in the dining room – a formal area we only used to dine in twice a year: Christmas and Boxing Days. Every other meal was in the kitchen. The dining table had all sorts of other uses: Ava did her dressmaking on it, Shawn made model aeroplanes on it and now I needed to work more seriously for school I did my homework there. I would be able to set up and leave my stuff out all week.

I heard a car on the drive; it was Patrick. I never knew his surname; he was simply known as Doctor Patrick to his patients and just Patrick to his friends. He had a strong Irish accent that I found difficult to understand, made even worse after he'd had a drink which was often the case before, during and after his visits.

"I've come to see your pa," he bellowed when he saw me open the door. I guessed he had already had a shot or two so just smiled and led the way down the long corridor to the study.

When we got there Bill asked me to fetch a couple of glasses and the whisky bottle. I ran up to the drinks cupboard, collected the requested things and went straight back with them. I put them on the desk and left, leaving the door slightly ajar behind me. A few seconds later, I was only halfway up the corridor when I heard it click shut. A visit from Patrick was usually going to involve a long, private discussion about Bill's health together with a lot of drinking. Of course, I'd already decided to listen in but first I went back to the dining room and spread my work out across the table just in case.

When I returned, I only needed to go down the corridor a little to hear as Patrick's voice boomed out like he was using a megaphone.

"I'm going to put you on a different drug. It's fairly new in being used as a treatment for MS but I think it's worth a try. See if we can get you a bit more comfortable."

Then I couldn't quite catch what Bill said but Patrick replied in an even more animated way,

"Look, Bill, how long have we known each other? Years. And I've been your doctor all that time as well, so you will just have to trust me. I know what I'm doing. I'll put you on this new drug for three months and if that hasn't made any difference then we'll think again. You are of course at liberty to get another opinion but I can already tell you it would be a waste of time. Everyone is different with their symptoms, so you shouldn't compare yourself to others. You should however be prepared for things to get worse. I would recommend sorting out your affairs early and planning for reduced mobility over the next few years."

I didn't stay to listen to any more. It was upsetting to hear the bad prospects. I'd already noticed Bill's decline and to think it would only get worse was difficult to accept. I went back to my homework area, and although I had plenty I should be getting on with, I was unable to concentrate.

Later on I heard Patrick leave, and Bill came in to see what we should choose for dinner. Needless to say we over ordered enormously, and had crispy duck and pancakes, chilli beef, sweet and sour chicken, rice and stir-fry, and despite feeling a little queasy at one point, we ate all of it. I cleared the plates away and Bill went to sit in the lounge to watch TV. He liked to catch the news most evenings, but was usually asleep in the chair straight after the headlines.

I joined him just before the news. As Ava was away I sat in her chair as it was more comfortable than the old sofa. The lounge, just like the rest of the house was a random collection of furniture and styles. Bill sat in a plastic garden chair; he liked it because you could adjust the back and feet by lifting the arms, so he could recline and nod off to sleep with his feet up. Ava's chair was the most recent purchase; it had huge arm rests, a deep purple velvet cover, and was so soft to sit in it felt like a giant hug. It smelt of her perfume, and I wondered how she was getting on in Cornwall as I curled into a ball inside it. Bill was beginning to drop off to sleep, making little snuffles and snorting sounds then suddenly opening his eyes as if nothing had happened.

The headlines started – GONG! – "More than one million demonstrate in Beijing," – GONG! – "Major work of art stolen from The National Gallery," – GONG!…What? An art robbery? I cast my mind back to the conversation between Ed and Bill and my heart was racing to hear the details. I noticed even Bill sat up in his dreamy state to listen. I pretended to not really be paying attention and curled deeper inside the chair.

"En route to The National Gallery with the Goya works for their new collection, a van was intercepted and the guards were forced at gunpoint to reveal the contents of the delivery. The perpetrators got away with a painting worth over a million pounds. Anyone with any information has been asked to contact the police directly."

Once the report was over Bill started to giggle. "What are you laughing at?" I asked innocently.

"Oh just something an old friend told me about that painting," he replied in a non-committal way.

I left it but I knew what this meant. Ed had pulled it off. One of the biggest art heists in history and Bill had funded it! I felt quite excited to be part of it, but also worried about the implications if Ed was ever caught. For now though I enjoyed our secret moment of fame on the television, knowing more than even the reporters and police did. I wondered where Ed was now. Was he at home also watching this on the TV? Had he already given it to Nicholas to start work on the copy? I couldn't wait to find out.

CHAPTER 6

On Sunday we went to Bill's brother's for the afternoon. My cousins were all out this time, so I was doubly bored. Then we started the long week of me going to work with Bill. I took my rucksack with my homework and set up at Bill's desk. He didn't often actually sit at his desk, but spent most of the time patrolling the showroom and approaching potential customers. Richard was also there operating as a salesman, desperate to please Bill and make up for his kindness. He winked at me through the glass partitions, and I thought he was looking more like his old smiley self. I was relieved Bill had managed to sort the mess out, although a few friends had asked him where Billie-Joe was recently. I had heard him lie that he'd taken off backpacking with some new girlfriend, so life went on.

It got to Friday evening and I started to pack up my things; everyone had left the showroom, and only Bernie remained locking up the mechanics' area. Bill had turned all the lights off, and locked up everything except the front door. The usual routine. Soon Bernie would come and collect his dog then we would all leave together, and Bill would set the alarm and lock the final door.

Suddenly I heard the front door open, and a group of three men with almost shaven heads bowled in. Bill began to say he had closed for the day, but the front man just interrupted him. "Dave said you have something that belongs to us. Let's go have a conversation in your office." Two of the men remained by the door, and the third man walked towards the offices, where I was standing. He didn't see me though, as it was nearly dusk now and all the lights were switched off. I didn't like the look of him as he approached, so I ducked under the desk with my rucksack to hide. He walked in; Bill had followed him demanding to know what this was about. I saw Bill through the crack nervously looking at his desk, obviously wondering where I was.

"I'm trying to locate something that belongs to me. The last thing I managed to get out of Dave was your name," the man said to Bill gruffly.

"What do you mean, *the last thing*?" Bill replied. He was always so confident and used to people looking up to him; this was the first time I'd heard his voice sound anxious.

"Let's just say I don't think you'll be doing business together again," the man answered curtly. "Now I've had a look around your place here and I can't see what I'm looking for. Where's the container, Bill?"

Oh God, the container in the garden, I thought…with the guns. The thought of it again scared me and I felt my heart thumping so hard I was worried they could hear it.

"I have no idea what you are talking about," said Bill. "I think you should leave."

The man smiled. He didn't say a word but quietly reached into his jacket and pulled out a gun. Bill put his hands up and started to back out of the office. The man pointed the gun at the old dog and without flinching pulled the trigger. The sound was like an immense thunder clap right above my head. My hands shot up to my mouth to try to keep the shocked noise in. I was compelled to look at the dog but my eyes filled with water, so I could hardly see. I could just make out his head lying on the floor at a strange angle, a black pool beginning to flood round it. His eyes were open: he was dead. Despite being in complete shock, instinct kicked in, and I knew to remain invisible there under the desk. My hand moved from across my face to inside my mouth. I bit down on my fist to stop any noise coming out; I didn't even blink in case my teardrops made a sound.

The man now turned the gun to point at Bill. "Are you sure you don't know what I'm looking for?" he asked once more.

Bill looked completely white but quickly managed to reply, "There's no need for anyone to get hurt; I'll get your container to you. Where do you want it taken to?"

The man sniggered. "There, that wasn't so hard, was it? Of course no one needs to get hurt. We'll simply follow you in our van to the container now, take our stuff back tonight, and be on our way. Let's go." He flicked the gun towards the front door as if to usher Bill in that direction.

"Yes, yes, sure I-I-just need to get my keys from the desk," Bill stammered, and he inched past the man, and back into the office, and around to my side of the desk. He opened the top drawer, and pretended to move things around as if looking for something. The man stayed in the doorway waiting. Bill didn't look down at me but simply made a halt sign with his hand below the desk, shut the drawer, walked back around the desk, and said, "Right, let's go."

I stayed there listening to them leave, and the lock clicking in the front door. I waited while I heard Bill's car start, and then a large engine rev before very slowly peeping through the glass wall to see the car pull away followed by a large van. They had gone. The place was silent.

Then I heard the mechanics' door open, and I saw Bernie creep out. I had completely forgotten he was still there. Why hadn't he come to help? I stood up straight so he would see me, then I looked at his dog's lifeless body behind the door. I moved past it gritting my teeth, trying not to look, but not quite managing. I had to avoid stepping in the blood which was now soaking into the carpet tiles. Even in the dull evening light I could make out where the bullet had blasted into him, shattering part of his head. I gently closed the door behind me so Bernie wouldn't have to see. "Don't go in there," I managed to say to him before bursting into tears.

Bernie tried to console me, and although he wasn't very good at it, and he smelt horrible, I sobbed into his anorak as if he was my only friend in the world. After a few moments he slowly pulled away and looked at me. "Where's your dad?" He glanced at Bill's office, moving towards the entrance.

"Don't go in!" I shouted through the tears. It was too late; Bernie opened the door and saw the horrific sight of his beloved pet on the office floor. He sank to the ground and tried to pick up the animal but it was a big old thing and all he could manage was to drag it onto his lap, cradling the old dog in his arms on the floor and crying, blood getting all over his coat. How useless he was crying like a baby when Bill was out there with those maniacs. "Bernie, we need to go now. We need to save Bill. I know where they have taken him. You need to take me home."

"Are you mad?" he wept. "We need to call the police!"

"NO!" I yelled. I knew that if we involved the police Bill would get in trouble. The guns were stored on his property after all. Whether he knew what was in that container or not he would be arrested. "We can't get Bill into trouble. He'll give them what they want, and that will be the end of it," I told him defiantly.

But Bernie wasn't listening, he was just rocking on the ground hugging his dead dog and wailing. His wife and daughter had been killed in a car crash years before I knew him, and the old dog was his last reminder of them. But I knew I couldn't get home without him; it was a twenty-minute drive away. I was going to have to wait for Bill to come back for me, and try to prevent Bernie calling the police in the meantime. I knew he would come back; he signalled with his hand for me to wait so that's what I should do.

What seemed like hours passed. Bernie had cried himself to exhaustion and was now slumped lifeless next to the furry body on the floor; congealed blood covered his hands and coat, and he looked awful. I had found a large old cardboard box and an old blanket for Bernie to wrap the dog in when he woke up. I tried to make the box look as nice as possible. I used my colouring pens to write

Troy's name on the side and drew flowers around it. He could take him home and bury him in his own garden.

Although I was worried what was going on back at my home, I had to remain positive. Bill would come back for me; I knew he would. I was hungry and tired and it was getting cold now the heating had gone off but still I focused on Bill sorting everything out. Eventually, I heard a car pull up outside, and very soon a key in the door. Bill burst in, calling out for me.

"I'm here!" I called out, so relieved to see him back in one piece. It was completely dark now and Bill was carrying a torch. Bernie roused and got up off the floor. He looked like he had aged ten years: his eyes were all puffy and his greasy hair, which was usually combed across the top of his head, had become knotted and messy.

He lunged at Bill. "Look at Troy! What happened? Where have you been?"

"Calm down, Bernie. I'm so sorry about Troy; they thought he was my dog and were trying to hurt me. It's all sorted now. No one else will get hurt." He looked over at me with such concern on his face as he spoke. I pushed the box towards Bernie. "I made a little coffin while you were sleeping. Look – it says Troy on the side, and I found a warm blanket to wrap him in so you can take him home."

Bill could see Bernie was overwhelmed with emotion and quickly said, "That's really kind; let's put Troy in it now so you can get off home, Bernie. We'll discuss this when you are feeling better. Take next week off and I'll call round to your place on Monday. Don't talk to anyone about this, Bernie. Do you understand?"

He put the blanket on the ground next to the dog and helped Bernie wrap him up and place him gently in the box. He closed the top and carried the box out to Bernie's car. Bernie followed in silence. I watched them from the front door, but I couldn't hear what was said. Then Bernie started the car and drove off into the night. Bill came back to me.

"Let's go home," he said. I picked up my rucksack and went to get into the car while Bill locked up again. He got into the driving seat beside me. "I'm very proud of you. That must have been very frightening to witness. You held it together remarkably and the little coffin you made for Troy was really lovely. Those men were nothing to do with me; just someone I knew got involved with them. Did you see the big green crate in our garden? It was full of things that belonged to those men; that's what they were looking for." He tried to say it all so casually, but I could detect his nerves. "They have it all back now, so they won't be bothering us again." He sounded like he was trying to convince himself rather than me. "Just try to forget all about it. I don't think it would help to tell Mum. We wouldn't want to upset her, would we?" He glanced over at me nervously whilst driving through the night. He didn't know I had been inside the container, or what I had taken, and I was praying the men didn't realise either. They knew where we lived now after all and I didn't think they were the kind to let me off.

I desperately wanted to know what had happened to Dave but I couldn't bring myself to ask, so I just said,

"No, I don't think we should worry Mum." I made the decision to learn how to use my gun so I could access it at all times, so I would be ready if I ever saw those men again. Although I felt frightened by the evening's events, I saw that it was time for me to toughen up if I wanted to survive in this world.

It was very late when we got home, and although exhausted, I was also starving, so I made us a sandwich. We ate in silence. Then Bill said he would clear up and I should just go to bed. I went upstairs, bolting the front door on my way, something we never did normally. Once in bed I kept the side lamp on and quietly sobbed into the pillow until I was asleep.

When I woke up it was gone ten. I jumped up, put on my dressing gown and went downstairs not believing it was so late. There was a used cereal bowl in the sink, and I could smell coffee. Bill had managed to sort out his own breakfast at least. I made myself some toast and orange juice and sat down at the table. The house was so quiet and I felt very alone. I wondered where Bill was when suddenly there was a bang on the window and I knocked my juice over with fright. It was just a clumsy bird: Ava had put a feeder outside, so she could watch the wildlife. I mopped up the drink, calmed at the realisation. Ava and Shawn would be back later today, and I needed to pull it together, so they didn't suspect anything.

After I cleared up and got dressed I went outside into the garden. I needed to see for myself what had happened to the container. As I went around the back of the garage I saw it was still there, the door unbolted and left ajar. I peeped inside; it was completely empty: a hollow metal box with absolutely no evidence left behind of what had been inside just hours before. I heard footsteps behind me. I turned in triple speed but it was just the gardener, Tony.

"Whena isa ... the ... boxa goina? Isa spoilt ... a ... grass," he tried to ask me.

I looked at him with relief. "Soon, I guess, as it's empty now," I replied as I walked away. I really did hope it was going to be taken away as well, so I could forget all about it.

I spent the morning aimlessly walking around outside, visiting my old favourite spots for spying. I was too grown up to be playing outside in them now. I found an old mud pie I had made ages ago and wondered why I had always liked making them so much; it held no interest for me now. I went back into the house to make lunch. It would be the last meal I was responsible for before Ava was due home. I heard Bill's voice; he was on the phone in the study. I could hear him from all the way up in the hall. He sounded angry. It wasn't often you heard him raise his voice; he always just had an unquestioning demeanour of authority about him that meant everyone automatically obeyed him first time.

"I want it taken away NOW! I don't care how you do it, just make it happen," he shouted, then I heard the phone receiver crash down onto its base. I hoped he was talking about the container. I don't know how it got there in the first place but it must have required some kind of crane and truck to lift it; Bill must be organising its removal.

I went into the kitchen and made the lunch. We were down to the last of the supplies now, so I opened a can and made tuna and cucumber sandwiches. Ava was going to have to do a big shop when she got home. I called Bill when it was ready. He sent me to fetch his pills then we sat and ate in silence. His face had an expression of burden across it as though he had the worries of the world on his shoulders. I tried to take his mind off things.

"I got eighty-nine per cent in my art project last term. Miss Avery says I should go to art college when I finish school," I said perkily.

"Good for you," was all he could manage with such a brief smile and glance in my direction I almost missed it. The silence continued. I finished eating and got up from the table, washed up the plates then said I had homework to finish and excused myself.

I was relieved to get away from the quiet. I went to my bedroom and put on some loud rock music, then lay down on the bed and closed my eyes. I must have dropped off for a moment as I was suddenly aware of my door opening and Shawn standing there. They had arrived back from Cornwall, and he was desperate to show off about how they had gone horse riding, and walked on the edge of a cliff, and eaten out in a restaurant. All the time he was rabbiting on I was thinking that was nothing compared to the week I'd had, except of course I couldn't mention any of it to anyone. I was going to have to keep it all bottled up inside forever.

Shawn soon got bored when I didn't give much of a response and left my room to go and call his friends. I went downstairs; Ava was in the kitchen with Bill. She was flying around the cupboards with a notepad writing down a long shopping list ready to replenish all the food we had eaten. Bill still sat silently at the table.

"Hello, darling!" she said as soon as she saw me. She tried to give me a hug but I remained rigid and didn't hug back. "What have you two been up to this week?" she asked with her hands on her hips. "Looking at your miserable faces I bet you wish you'd come to Cornwall with me now!"

Bill glanced at me. I knew he was willing me to pull it together, so I said, "I think the chicken we ate last night was off. I forgot to put it back in the fridge the day before and it's given me a stomach ache."

"Oh no, silly girl. You should know about food safety," Ava replied crossly. She took food hygiene very seriously – even more so in her current diet, fitness, and exercise fad. "Bill, do you feel ill as well?"

Bill agreed he wasn't feeling great and that little lie relieved us from any further grilling from Ava. It actually made her feel quite important to think we couldn't manage without her even for a week.

CHAPTER 7

The next day it was back to school as usual. Everyone was talking about what they had done during the half-term holiday. I was still in my bubble about my experience, and not able to share it, so just said I'd been ill all week. Only my friend Harriet wasn't convinced with my story.

"I thought you had to cook for your dad all week while your mum was away. Did you still have to go into work with him while you were ill?" she asked in a disbelieving way in front of everyone.

"Yes, well it was just a sort of headache illness, so I had to sit in the office all day and rest," I responded. It was clear she didn't believe me, and now nor did anyone else. They all walked off together whispering and giving me disapproving looks. Girls could be so cruel.

I spent the rest of the day by myself, eager for the bell to signify home time. Eventually it rang, and I ducked outside quickly to avoid any more black looks or confrontations. Ava was always early to pick me up, so I knew she would be waiting. I spotted her car, and immediately leapt in the passenger seat. She didn't give me her usual 'pleased to see me' look but just started the car, and pulled away towards home. It wasn't until we were on the main road she began to speak.

"We've had some bad news today." She paused for a moment to make sure she had my attention. Our little car journeys seemed to be the only time we conversed now; she had me trapped as her only audience. "You know Bernie from the garage who worked for Dad for years? He was found dead this morning. He'd hanged himself." Ava started to weep. "Apparently his old dog Troy passed away last week, and as he was the last connection to his family I guess he just didn't see the point of carrying on any more. He'd been depressed for years, and Dad has been trying to support him for ages." Tears were flowing down her cheeks now. She carried on about how Bill had gone over to Bernie's house after he hadn't turned up for work and found him. The police said he'd been dead for at least twenty-four hours.

She stopped talking for a second and all I could say was, "Oh that's awful." I'm not sure it sounded convincing, but I was so shocked I couldn't muster up any more words.

The vision of Bernie's stout body hanging lifeless appeared in my head. I imagined his eyes bulged open, just staring, and his black, greasy hair dangling over his forehead as he swayed like a pendulum. I imagined Bill's face as he found him. How did he get in? Did he see through a window and smash it? Or had Bernie left the front door unlocked knowing Bill had planned the visit, and wanting him to be the one to discover his body?

"The police have been interviewing his colleagues all day, but it's just protocol. It's clear it was suicide. Such a shame, poor Bernie." Ava cried. I don't know why she was so upset; she couldn't stand the man when he was alive. If anyone had cared about him this wouldn't have happened. I remained silent for the rest of the journey. Now Bernie was dead there were no witnesses to what happened, I thought. I wasn't upset. Dazed perhaps, but not upset. I wondered if he'd buried Troy in the little coffin I'd made.

"He left a note, apparently," Ava finished off as we pulled into our drive.

"What did it say?" I perked up with interest.

"He thanked Bill for looking after him all these years, and that he mustn't blame himself. Well, I should think not! Bill's not to blame!" Ava said as she wrenched on the hand brake. "Come on, I need to start the dinner." She got out of the car, wiped her face and went inside the house. Seemed like she had got over the news after all.

Bill didn't come home for dinner. Ava and Shawn talked about Bernie, and theorised about why he'd done it. I just stayed mute, and ate wishing they would change the subject. In my bedroom after dinner I took out my gun; it didn't seem so heavy any more. I'd filled the magazine with bullets and practised loading and unloading it into the handle of the gun many times. I loaded it and pulled back the slide so a bullet engaged into the chamber, primed to be fired out and sat in front of the mirror looking at myself. Releasing the safety catch, I put my finger on the trigger, and I held the gun up next to my head, looking straight into my own eyes. If I was going to kill myself this is how I'd do it. But not here. I'd go to some remote place on the top of a cliff and pull the trigger, leaving my body to fall way down into the water below, never to be found, washed away forever. It's a coward's way out to leave yourself for others to deal with the aftermath, as Bernie did.

The rest of the school term dragged on. Although I'd become a bit of a loner in the class, I wasn't afraid of conflict and could easily stand my ground in any arguments or fights. Once a girl I didn't like, and who I'd had several disagreements with, attempted to knock me over during a hockey game. After a quick glance to check the teacher wasn't looking, I took a swing at her head with the hockey stick and managed to chip one of her front teeth. Her face swelled up like she had the hockey ball in her mouth. Blood poured down her chin as she looked at me in utter disbelief. After this particular incident no one dared to mess with me. Even the teachers seemed to avoid clashing with me, and as long as I handed in my work on time I had a quiet life.

The only place I felt comfortable was the Art room. Miss Avery continued to praise my artistic efforts and gave me extra tuition during lunch break. She liked me. I didn't feel she had any ulterior motive other than to nurture my talent and be my friend. I also noticed she didn't go and sit in the staffroom with all the other teachers, so I felt we were well suited. She told me about her life and her difficult upbringing, and gained my trust. In return, I divulged a bit on how I'd been feeling. Before the end of term she gave me her home phone number and said I could call any time during the summer holidays. She proposed we could even go out for a picnic and sketching trip and she could give me some extra tuition if my parents agreed.

I was keen on that idea. I ran it past Ava and she was happy for me to go, as long as it wasn't during the last week in July as that was when she had planned a family holiday to Cornwall. Bill was frightened of flying so if we ever went away it would be in the car. I never particularly enjoyed the trips. I always felt car sick and Bill would never stop the car for a break. This year the plan was to stay in a four-star hotel with a swimming pool, all meals included and a weekly gala dinner and dance. Maybe it wouldn't be too bad getting away from everything that had happened.

The first few weeks of the school holidays passed quite quickly. As Ava didn't work she was around all the time, keen to try to do things 'together'. One of her favourite things was to go for a bike ride. I had never found riding a bike particularly enjoyable and had therefore been left with a rather dated fold-up bicycle which was very slow. Shawn on the other hand loved cycling and had been given a racing bike for his last birthday. If the three of us ever went out together I was always about a mile behind him with Ava in the middle trying to keep up with Shawn, but not leaving me behind.

"Fancy a bike ride?" Ava's beaming face appeared at the lounge doorway. I was quite happily watching TV and I knew behind the door she was already dressed in her Lycra cycling shorts and was going to go whatever my answer. Shawn's head popped up behind her. Looking at me he shook his head silently as if to suggest he didn't want me to go as I would just slow him down.

"No, I'm just watching this," I replied.

"Okay, see you in a bit," Ava said and darted off with Shawn.

I knew she wouldn't force me to go. Earlier that week I had started my period. I had to go and tell her as I had run out of products. She simply gave me a pack of her brick-like sanitary towels and sent me off to the bathroom. For someone that was desperate for my attention, she certainly didn't like discussing anything that didn't fit her own agenda. Still, it was just one more obstacle I would have to face alone. As soon as I could get into a town I would buy myself some tampons, I thought; it might have to wait until I saw Miss Avery, but she'd help me out.

They had been gone about an hour when I heard a car on the drive. I looked out the hall window to see Bill's car followed by another one. I squinted to see who was driving; it was Ed. I hadn't heard anything more about the art robbery and was eager to find out about it. I knew once they got in the house, Bill would call out to see if anyone was home and if not just go down to the study. He wasn't capable of making a drink himself, so they would simply go without.

I remembered the old hiding hole I had made in the study cupboard...could I still fit in? There wasn't time to think; I darted down the corridor to the study and slid open the cupboard. It was exactly as I had left it; I knew no one ever looked in there. I squeezed into the central hole, knocking over a couple of the box files. I was quite a bit bigger now and it was too small a space. I heard Bill shout, "Anyone home?" from the hall. They would only be a few seconds away from entering the study. I slid the door closed, but didn't have time to replace the box files around me. If they opened the cupboard I would be discovered. I heard laughing as they entered the room. "When I saw it on the news I just couldn't believe it!" Bill was saying. "You actually pulled it off."

"It gets better," Ed replied. "Just wait until you see what Nicholas has achieved!"

I heard some things being moved about in the room and quite a lot of rustling.

"Even I struggle to tell the difference. I have marked the box of the fake one with a tiny dot, see? Otherwise I don't think even I could tell which is which! Let's put them side by side on the desk and see if you can tell," Ed said.

Then a bit more noise before Bill said, "I'm seeing double. How on earth did he do it? I can't see any difference…that really is incredible. They are exactly the same! So what's the plan now?"

Ed said, "I have a buyer lined up. I'm meeting him tonight. No one knows about the forgery except you. I want you to keep it here – stick it in the loft or something. I can't risk it being discovered at my place, but at some point in the future we can sell it again. It's all agreed with Nicholas that I will keep it as my part of the deal, after expenses of course, and he will get the remaining profit from tonight's transaction."

"Hello!" Ava's voice called out from the hall. She was back with Shawn and on her way down to see who was in the study with Bill.

"Quick, let's go up to her before she comes in here," Bill said. "We'll come back in a minute to wrap them up."

I waited for them to leave the room and counted the steps for them to get up the corridor to the hall. I slid the cupboard door open and climbed out.

There on the desk were the two identical paintings, each in a perfectly constructed wooden container – about the size of a giant pizza box. I studied them; nothing separated them. I was surprised at how small they were as I had always imagined a much bigger painting. How can a painting this small be so valuable? I observed the images: in the foreground, a man dressed in black robes was refuelling an oil lamp while donkeys danced around behind him. They were very dark and lacked any bright colour and weren't in frames. I carefully picked one up and took it out of the box and turned it around – it looked aged on the back. I gently put it down and picked up the other one and turned it over. Again it looked exactly the same. I examined the box and there on the side was a tiny dot. This was the fake. I thought back to what Miss Avery had said about how to tell the age of a painting – oil paint takes years to dry out. I lifted it to my nose and took a deep sniff. There was only a faint smell of chemicals. I gently lowered it into its box and picked up the original again and sniffed. Nothing, it didn't smell of anything.

Ed wanted Bill to look after the forgery but surely the buyer wouldn't know the difference? I swapped the paintings around placing the forgery in the box without the dot and the original in the other one. After all it was Bill who had funded the robbery; why shouldn't he have the original? I heard voices coming. Quickly I scrabbled into my hiding spot. Ed and Bill came back in.

"Thanks for the offer of tea, I'd better get going now though," Ed said. Then more rustling noise as he must have been wrapping the paintings up again. "Here. Hide this. After this deal I'm going to be lying low for a bit, so keep it safe. Think of it as your guarantee that you will get your loan repaid back."

"Sure. No rush with the repayment. Keep safe, Ed, won't you?" Bill said. Then suddenly I heard the cupboard right next to me slide open and the light flooded in. If Bill looked slightly to the right he would see me; I didn't breathe but remained absolutely motionless praying I wasn't discovered. He placed the wooden box on top of the files on my right, then I saw a hand disappear and the door slid shut again. That was so close, I thought. Thank goodness he chose the other side to put the painting. I heard the study door close as they left the room, voices fading into the distance and out of the house.

I crept out again; I was sweating. I needed to get out of the study before my whereabouts were questioned, so I ran up the corridor and straight up the stairs to my room. I thought about what I had just done. A stolen work of art now sat in our house which no one knew the truth about but me.

CHAPTER 8

Ava spent the next week preparing for the holiday. The suitcases were brought out and dusted down ready for use. I was left with the smallest and oldest one with a broken lock on one side while Bill and Ava shared a big new leather one with buckles round it, and Shawn had their old one. Same old story: always the end in line for anything new. I had strict instructions to keep all the clothes I wanted to take clean, and only wear old things for the whole week before the departure. You would think we were going for a round-the-world cruise, not just a week in Cornwall. I carelessly packed my suitcase full of clothes and put my important things to keep with me at all times in my rucksack: my diary, Walkman, a couple of tapes, some pens and my loaded gun.

Finally, the car was packed and it was time to go. Shawn and I sat in the back with a case between us as we couldn't fit all the luggage in the boot of the Mercedes. Bill wanted to go via the business to have a final check on things, but Ava insisted that Richard would manage just fine for a week and Bill should trust him and not interfere. So the long four-hour journey to Cornwall began. Shawn kept pushing the case over to my side and before we had even driven out of the estate an argument had started. Ava's head twisted around and in her high-pitched voice she instructed us to behave. Shawn began explaining how it was all my fault when Bill flicked his eyes up into the rear-view mirror, and that one silent stare was enough to keep us quiet for the next four hours. He didn't stop for a break for the whole journey and when we finally arrived at The Langmoor Manor Hotel we were all hungry and bored. It was mid-afternoon and the receptionist told us that cream tea would be served in the lounge until five, so we had plenty of time to get settled into our rooms. The porter loaded the cases onto a trolley and took us up one floor in the lift.

"The smallest room is on this floor," he announced. "Number 212 just down the corridor, and round the corner." I took my case off the trolley while everyone else waited in the lift. "Here's the key; your parents' room is 459 on the fourth floor."

"We'll come and give you a knock on our way down to tea in a minute," Ava told me as the lift doors closed and I was left standing alone. I dragged my case along the mustard carpet to room 212. Just as I was unlocking the door I heard voices. An older boy and a girl who looked about my age were coming towards me. I glanced up at them with a nervous smile.

They both stopped. "Hey, have you just arrived?" the girl asked me. She had a very different accent, unlike anyone I knew. "My name's Kitty and this is my brother Dan. Can we have a look in your room? My room is number 219 and Dan's next door in 217. I expect you can see the pool from your window." I unlocked the door and Kitty pushed past me and went straight over to the window. Dan lingered in the doorway for a moment then picked up my case like it was just full of air, strutted into the room and put it on the bed for me. He was so cool. We shared a silent look at each other while Kitty continued to hang out the window nattering away and trying to catch a glimpse of the pool. "What's your name? How long are you staying? We've already been here a week and it's been so boring; we only have two days left now before we head back up to Liverpool and the pubs and some life! Absolutely nothing goes on here. Our parents have just lain by the pool for seven days leaving us to amuse ourselves. Now you are here we can have some fun! How old are you?" She stopped talking for a second for me to answer.

I wanted to say I was older than I was; I was quite tall for my age anyway, so I lied and said, "My name's Cat, I'm fifteen, you?"

"Oh, I'm fourteen and Dan is sixteen, so you are in the middle. That's funny; I'm Kitty and you're Cat! Come on, we'll show you around." Dan smiled at me again; he must have been pleased I was older than his sister, and I didn't think lying for just a couple of days would do any harm. Then there was a knock on the door and Ava walked in.

"Oh!" she exclaimed, seeing Dan first. "Who are you?"

"Hello!" boomed Kitty from behind me. "We are just going to explore the hotel together. Bye, nice to meet you." She shuffled past Ava and down the corridor closely followed by Dan. Ava stood there looking at me; she wasn't used to being talked to like that.

"Yeah, I'm going with them. They are going to show me around. I'll see you for dinner?" I asked with a newfound confidence. I needed to move fast before Dan was out of sight. I stepped out into the corridor, looking expectantly at Ava to also move out the room, which fortunately she did and I closed the door and put the key in my pocket. Ava remained in the corridor looking like she was deciding whether to refuse permission and make me go with her, or simply be content that I was busy for a bit.

I was already walking away when she said, "Okay, see you at six. Be careful."

I caught up with Kitty and Dan. They showed me through a side door leading to a staircase. Kitty slid down the banister and landed in the lobby. Dan and I followed side by side down the stairs, brushing arms occasionally and glancing at each other giggling. Kitty was waiting at the bottom, "Come on, you two!" She squeezed between us and linked arms with me pulling me away in her direction and away from Dan. We strutted off together. Kitty was certainly feisty and didn't want to be left out; she chatted continuously as she showed me all the facilities the hotel had to offer: mini golf, swimming pool, gardens and an outside bar. She pointed out the lane that led down to the beach and said she wasn't allowed to go down there without telling her parents first. After a while I noticed Dan had disappeared, so I took the opportunity to quiz her about him.

"Has Dan got a girlfriend?" I dropped in at one point.

"No, oh! Ew! You don't fancy him do you?" Kitty looked repelled, then immediately decided it was okay and said, "I think you two would make a cute couple."

We found ourselves back at the poolside, and Kitty saw her parents. It wasn't particularly sunny out, but they were both lying on sunbeds with just their swimming costumes on. "Come on; I'll introduce you." She grabbed my hand and we ran over to them. Her mother greeted me in such a welcoming way – quite the opposite to how Ava had greeted Kitty earlier.

"I'm so pleased Kitty has found a friend to play with, even if it is just for a couple of days. You two run along and have fun now," she said finally as she closed her eyes and settled back in the lounger, clearly ready for a rest having been disturbed for long enough. We went over to the pool, took off our shoes and socks and sat on the edge swishing our feet in the water. I was quite pleased to have someone to talk to and Kitty was so easy going; the conversation just kept moving. Eventually I noticed almost all the sunloungers were empty. Everyone must be starting to get ready for dinner. I looked at my watch.

"I'm going to have to go and get ready for dinner. I'll see you tomorrow, yeah? Maybe try to bring Dan along?"

"Oh yeah okay; I'll ask him. Check with your parents if it's okay to go down to the beach and bring your swimming costume. Meet me here at ten," she called after me.

I ran off to my room. There was only about ten minutes to get ready. I rummaged through my suitcase; now I knew Dan would be in the dining room I wished I had brought entirely different clothes with me. What did

I own that would impress him? I settled on a puffball skirt and top with my ballet pumps, the most feminine outfit I had packed, ran a brush through my hair and went back downstairs to find my family. They were already in the bar area. Ava was sipping a Bacardi and Coke, Bill had a pint of Guinness and Shawn had a massive grin on his face as he had been allowed a shandy. They were talking to a younger couple.

When I pitched up and Ava saw I was wearing a skirt for a change she was delighted. She introduced me to their new friends, Steve and Jo; they had been away for nearly a week already and were heading home the next afternoon. I took an immediate liking to Jo. She was tall and slim, and had the best taste in clothes – she was wearing a tight pair of trousers with red patent high heels and a silk blouse that just floated around as she moved. Her hair was naturally wavy and her lips were painted a vibrant red to match her shoes and nails. Steve was more ordinary looking in a suit the same as all the other men in the room, including Bill and Shawn. Bill and Steve were talking business while Ava and Jo were deep in a conversation about children.

"I've always wanted a daughter; you are so lucky to have such a beautiful offspring, Ava." Jo gave me a broad smile and continued, "I bet you go on wonderful shopping trips together and go and have coffee and cakes before seeing a film at the cinema!" Her eyes grew wide at the thought of such fun and she moved along the sofa a bit and patted the space to indicate I could sit next to her. "So Catherine, what's your favourite thing to do?" she asked me, but before I could answer Shawn interrupted, "She likes to spy on people."

"Oh yes, me too. I love people-watching from a café on the street; I could sit for hours just imagining what's going on in their lives," Jo said dreamily. I liked her even more now she had taken my side over Shawn's. "Maybe, if Ava doesn't mind, I could borrow you tomorrow? I need to select a present for my niece – she's about your age and I haven't a clue what to get her. We could walk into the village and have a look around. I know it's only a short walk up the road and there's only one or two shops there, but Steve has arranged to play tennis, so I'll need a thing to do in the morning before we head home after lunch." She looked directly at Ava and patiently waited for an answer. Ava looked a bit thrown at this random stranger asking to take her daughter out for a walk.

"Oh, I'd love to but I thought I might go down to the beach with Kitty tomorrow," I said in my most polite voice.

Ava cast me a look; I knew she didn't like Kitty. "No, we'll all go to the beach together another time. You can go with Jo to the village, just for the morning; we were going to have a pool day tomorrow anyway."

"Good, that's settled then; I'll see you in the morning." Jo gave my leg a squeeze as she got up. "Steve, it's time to go through to the dining room; mustn't miss our slot."

I felt like I'd just been sold. Why would I want to go for a walk with a stranger? Jo seemed nice enough but it was a bit weird. How had she managed to wrap Ava around her finger so fast? She was certainly an expert at getting what she wanted. Now I wouldn't be able to spend the day with Dan and it was all Ava's fault. Why did she have to ruin everything? After tomorrow Dan would only have one whole day left and I bet Ava would drag me out somewhere then too. Bill looked over at me, oblivious to the deal that had just been struck. "Cheer up, Cat, you're on holiday."

CHAPTER 9

The next morning before going down to breakfast, I went to knock on Kitty's door. I hadn't seen her or her family at dinner, and I thought it best to tell her I wasn't allowed to go to the beach. She didn't take the news well.

"Why not? You're fifteen! I was relying on you to come, so I could go!"

"Why can't Dan take you?" I asked.

"He won't come if you're not coming," she shouted as she shut the door in my face.

I stood there a little stunned. No one had ever slammed a door at me. A couple of guests opened their doors and peeped out at the noise. "Everything's fine," I murmured as I began to head back down the corridor. Dan's door opened, and an overwhelming smell of aftershave floated out. "Hey," he simply said. His shirt was undone, and he was wearing shorts and flip-flops.

"Oh hey," I replied. I felt my cheeks start to burn. "I can't come to the beach today; I have to go into the village."

"Sure. No worries," he said. "Have fun." He smiled and closed his door.

I was alone again in the corridor. Great, I thought. Rejected again.

I went down for breakfast. Ava was at the buffet counter picking out the pineapple from the fruit salad bowl. Bill was at the table reading the paper and waiting for his full English to arrive. Shawn was just eating everything haphazardly: some toast, then yogurt, a sort of cake thing and then some sausage. I went and fetched myself a bowl of Coco Pops and sat down. We all ate our food of choice and although we knew Ava didn't approve there was nothing she could do about it for a change. Once we had all finished Bill gave me a £5 note.

"Just in case you want anything in the village," he said. "Remember to check your change and come and find us by the pool when you get back."

What was I going to get with a fiver? That wouldn't even be enough for a coffee. I thanked him through gritted teeth, said my goodbyes and went to meet Jo in the reception. There she was, looking just as glamorous as the evening before. She was sitting in a shaft of sunlight, wearing a short flowery dress, her tanned legs crossed and sunglasses so big you could hardly see any of her face.

"Darling, good morning!" she said as I came into view. "You look gorgeous!"

How could I look gorgeous? I was just wearing some jeans shorts and a T-shirt and carrying my worn rucksack. It felt good for such enthusiasm over my appearance for a change though and I gave her a big smile.

"Come on, let's hit the town!" she said as she linked my arm and together we strutted out of the front door of the hotel and towards the road.

We walked along the lane for a few minutes, Jo sashaying along in her wedges quizzing me about my home and school. We came to a small turning and Jo said this was a nicer walk to the village off the main road. After a few moments a two-door sports car pulled up beside us; we looked across to see Steve was driving. He lowered the passenger window.

"Hi you two, fancy a lift? My tennis was cancelled and I thought I could drive you into town instead of just the village, so you can have a look round the proper shops."

"Wonderful, darling!" Jo said, and she opened the passenger door, and pulled the seat forward, so I could climb in the back.

"Oh, er…it's okay, I think I should probably just walk back to the hotel," I stammered. It didn't feel quite right to get in their car.

Steve wrenched on the hand brake, but left the engine running and got out to come around to my side of the car.

"Come on, I'll bring you back to the hotel before lunch," he said as he took my arm and steered me towards the open door.

"No, thank you." I tried to wriggle away but his grip tightened and he forced me into the back of the car. Jo flipped the seat back and got in and shut the door. Suddenly Steve was back in the driving seat, and we were moving away.

"What are you doing? I don't want to go!" I shouted. I could feel tears forming in my eyes. This didn't feel right. "Take me back to the hotel!"

Jo leaned around. "Calm down. We are not going to hurt you, darling; it's just that after talking to your lovely parents last night it seems they have quite a lot of money, so we thought we'd just borrow you for a bit. I'm sorry to disappoint you, Catherine, but I tricked you. I don't even have a niece. Try not to worry. We're just going for a little drive first then we'll call your parents and you will be back safe and sound in no time."

They had been lying all along. Lying about pretending to like me. Lying about the present for their niece. They had tricked Ava into letting me go and now they were kidnapping me for money! Amidst the feeling of panic about what was happening I also felt a burning rage. I was fed up with being used. They were not going to take me away. I needed to think fast. The car was moving quickly and I didn't know where we were going; it wouldn't be long before we would be too far away from the hotel for me to find my way back. I pretended to start sobbing and bent forward, gently opening my rucksack and ever so slowly reaching inside for my gun. There it was, the familiar security I had become accustomed to handling. With my left arm I grabbed Jo around the neck while putting the gun to her temple with my right.

"Stop the fucking car or I'll blow her fucking brains out!" I yelled. I was shaking but resolute, adrenalin pumping now and an overwhelming feeling like I was in some kind of unrealistic blockbuster movie.

Steve looked over in absolute disbelief. "What the ... that's not a real gun. You don't have a real gun," he half laughed.

"I said, STOP THE CAR!" I sounded frantic as I pushed the end of the gun right into the side of Jo's head.

Still Steve continued driving, so I pulled back the slider to engage a bullet.

That did the trick. "Steve," Jo stammered. "Steve, let's pull over and sort this out."

Steve pulled over and stopped the car. We were still on the country road and there were no other vehicles around. I let go of Jo's neck and pointed the gun at Steve. "Do you want me to show you how real it is?" I tempted him. He looked more carefully at the gun; I could see some reservations on his face. "Now, let me out the car," I said again, aggressively kicking at the back of Jo's seat.

Jo looked across nervously at Steve. She opened her door and got out. Glancing at me in the back she pulled the seat forward, so I could get out. I signalled for her to move away. She moved several paces back and I jumped out with my bag. Steve stayed put in the driver's seat. I pointed the gun at her again and ushered her back to the car.

Neither of them said a word; they just looked completely dumbfounded. As soon as Jo was back in the car Steve sped off down the road. I stood there watching the car getting smaller and smaller until it eventually went around a corner and out of sight. I finally lowered the gun, my arms hanging limp by my side. My legs seemed to give way underneath me and I sank to the ground in a heap. It began to dawn on me what had just happened: I had escaped from being kidnapped. The gun had saved me. I looked down at it, my hands shaking. The feeling of power with this piece of metal in my hand was intense. I disarmed my weapon. At last, it was my turn to take charge.

After about ten minutes I put it carefully back in my rucksack and got to my feet. I should get back to the hotel and explain what happened. We must have driven at least a couple of miles, so I needed to get moving. Jo and Steve would be long gone by the time I could report them, and I didn't even know what make of car I had been in. Judging by how quickly they took us all in, they must have done this sort of thing before – low level con-artists looking for rich prey in holiday resorts. As I started walking back it struck me that of course I couldn't tell anyone. I would have to explain where I got the gun and I knew I couldn't tell the police about that.

By the time I had walked back to the hotel it was lunchtime. I had managed to calm down on the walk and come to the firm decision to keep the morning's turmoil to myself. My gun was too important to lose. I nipped up to my room to clean myself up and wash my face before heading down and locating Bill and Ava by the pool looking at the snack menu.

"Ah good, just in time. Did you choose a nice present for Jo's niece?" Ava asked me. "Where is Jo?"

I had to really sound convincing now, so they would drop the subject quickly. "Yes, I thought she would like a notebook and pen with a picture of the beach on. It took longer than we thought and when we got back Steve said he had been called to a meeting so they had to head straight off. Jo said to thank you and say her goodbyes. She was a bit of a pain actually and it was a boring morning. What have they got for lunch? I'm starving."

I knew Ava wouldn't bother pressing me for details but would simply be pleased I didn't hit it off with Jo. She was so easy to fool.

After lunch, I said I was going to fetch my swim things from the room, but I actually went to search for Dan and Kitty. After looking everywhere I could think of, I eventually spotted Shawn talking to Kitty by the tennis courts. I went up to them. "Hey."

"So now I get it," Kitty said maliciously. She obviously hadn't forgiven me yet. "You're not fifteen at all, but fourteen just like me. What a little liar." Oh no, Shawn had told her my age. Great. Now she'd hate me even more and tell Dan, and that would be the last time he'd think of me. "Is that why you made up some lame excuse about not coming to the beach?"

"No, no I really wasn't allowed," I burst out. "Let's go now; Shawn, you come too so the adults agree." I looked at Shawn in an attempt to appeal to him.

"Mm, let me think about it…are you worth it? Nope. I don't think so," he said and turned to walk off before adding, "By the way, I'd hurry up and get back to the pool and to Mummy and Daddy."

I looked back at Kitty, but she was already walking away. Disappointed, I went to my room, took my swim bag and went back to the pool. Ava and Bill had started talking to some other holidaymakers now. Were they gluttons for punishment or what? I settled on a lounger behind them, and sat back with my Walkman and headphones blaring out Guns N' Roses. I just wanted the holiday to end. I was still shaken up from the morning's traumatic events, and despite putting on a brave face for everyone, I just wanted to curl into a ball and disappear. After a while I saw the new holidaymaker writing down something and giving the note to Bill, so I turned my music off and tuned in to their conversation for a bit.

"He's the best doctor I've ever met. Cured Susan after a botched attempt by the NHS. I've put his Harley Street address on the paper as well as his number. Give him a ring and have a chat. I'll bet he'll do a scan rather than just more X-rays and hopefully get to the root of your problems."

Susan (I assume) spoke up then, "Yes, it's true, Bill; I had been going on with my diagnosis for a whole year before I changed doctors. Now that I am receiving the right treatment I'm feeling better. Cost a fair bit of course but my goodness it's worth it."

"Thanks," Bill said. "It's good to have a recommendation for someone new. I've been thinking for a while about getting a second opinion."

Ava rolled her eyes but just said, "Thank you, Thomas. We will definitely be giving Dr Bedson a ring. I'll tell him you sent us."

"Right. Time for a dip," said Thomas getting up and stripping down to his trunks. What a sight. Nothing worse than seeing too much old-man flesh. Susan joined Thomas in the pool and Ava carried on talking to Bill.

"I think we should call and make an appointment from the hotel reception. See if you can be seen in Harley Street as a matter of urgency; maybe they will have a slot next week."

"Yes, sure. Can you make the arrangements? I still feel bad about going behind Patrick's back," Bill said.

Ava got up. "I'm going right now." She slipped her heeled sandals on and wrapped a silk sarong around herself and swished off to the reception. She was on a mission. I knew the signs well. Ten minutes later she returned triumphant.

"Next Friday at two," she declared with a big satisfied grin on her face.

"Oh, that is quick," Bill said nervously.

"You get what you pay for," Ava replied as she settled back to her sun-worshipping position, despite the fact it was getting a bit chilly.

During dinner, I hoped to catch sight of Dan, but again I didn't spot him or Kitty there. I guess they weren't eating in the hotel. Ava told us her plans for the next day. We would be going to a nearby beach with a picnic from the hotel. As I'd already given up on having a good time and after my attempted kidnap I didn't object to the prospect of staying with Bill and Ava for a day.

The next morning we left straight after breakfast. We drove around the narrow lanes for about half an hour before finding the particular cove Ava wanted to go to. Once there, it wasn't as bad as I'd thought: messing about in the rock pools and dipping in and out of the sea, eating warm sandwiches and crisps, and getting a polystyrene cup of tea from the beach café. Even Shawn didn't annoy me and we returned to the hotel tired and hungry for dinner.

Later, I was in my room getting ready for bed; it was nearly ten when there was a soft knocking on my door. I assumed it would be Ava come to give me some instruction about the next day, so I just opened the door in my pyjamas without thinking. It wasn't Ava, it was Dan. I stood there looking uncomfortable, suddenly aware of what I must have looked like. I turned a bright red colour and just about managed to say, "Hi."

"Hey," Dan said. He smiled. "I'm off home tomorrow and I wanted to say goodbye." He leaned in and gave me the gentlest of kisses on my lips. "I enjoyed meeting you," he whispered as he pulled away and walked slowly back up the corridor, giving a tiny look behind him with a smile before disappearing into his room. I closed my door and threw myself on the bed with the biggest grin on my face for months. My heart eventually slowed down as I drifted off into a deep slumber. Maybe the holiday wasn't so bad after all.

CHAPTER 10

The rest of the holiday flew by without further incident and it wasn't long before it was our turn to pack up and go home. Almost as soon as we got back after the long arduous journey Ava was instructing us to separate our washing out into piles of smalls, whites and colours. I asked if I could call Miss Avery to arrange to go and do some drawing with her later in the week. Ava agreed if I unpacked everything first. That sped me up; I'd been planning to see Miss Avery since the end of term. I waited until Ava was busy upstairs so I could make the call in private; I hated her eavesdropping. We arranged to meet on Wednesday when she would pick me up at eleven and speak to Ava then as well. She asked if there was anything I liked to eat, so she could make a picnic. I was really looking forward to seeing her.

The next few days leading up to it were so boring. The container in the garden had miraculously disappeared whilst we had been away, Bill went back to work, Ava had masses of jobs and shopping to catch up on after the holiday, and Shawn was beginning to be out a lot more with his friends. Jack came round for his money as usual and Digger continued his secret meetings in the study with Bill. The only thing that had changed was that the police had stopped coming around looking for Billie-Joe. I still had flashbacks of what he had done, but I was pleased to hear Richard was getting on really well at the garage and he and April had decided to have one more go at IVF. Ava had been gossiping over tea with one of her friends about how they had managed to afford it so suddenly after the robbery, and I could almost see the cogs in her brain wondering if Richard did have anything to do with the theft after all. Little did she know that it was actually Bill funding the IVF. I wondered if she would gossip so much if she knew the truth.

Wednesday came around eventually and the weather looked good: a bright sunny day perfect for a picnic and a day out in the open. I had already packed my rucksack – my gun of course in the bottom, diary, notebook and pens, and then a few drawing pencils and an A4 sketchbook. It was on my back when Ava was suddenly behind me opening the top and trying to put a hat and cardigan inside. I whipped round as I felt her open it.

"What are you doing?" I yelled. "My bag is private!" I screamed without thinking.

"I was just putting you in a jumper in case it gets cold. What on earth have you got in there that's so secret?" Ava retorted.

"Nothing…sorry, thanks… I'll put it on now," I said quietly, instantly regretting my outburst as I took the jumper from her and moved away.

Just then Miss Avery pulled in the drive. "We'll discuss your attitude later," Ava called after me as I dashed out to meet her, but I knew the way Ava's mind worked and now she had a sniff of a potential secret something she would need to investigate further. As soon as the car stopped I jumped in the passenger seat. Miss Avery smiled and lowered the window to talk to Ava.

"I'll bring Catherine back by six, okay?" she said to Ava.

"Oh yes thank you, have a good time," Ava replied. I could tell she was a bit annoyed but didn't want to cause a scene in front of Miss Avery by telling me off and rooting through my bag in front of her and possibly finding nothing; she would save it for later. So we said our goodbyes and drove away. By the time we were out the drive I sensed she would be in my room snooping about looking for clues. Fortunately, my most prized and secret possession was with me.

Miss Avery drove for about an hour before stopping at a service station for a toilet break. She chatted a little on the way about what she had been doing in the holidays so far, and said I could call her Piper whilst we weren't in school. After a quick stop we carried on for another forty minutes before turning down a long bumpy track, where eventually she pulled up the car on the verge and stopped. I looked around; we didn't seem to be anywhere special. There were no other cars or people around.

"Come on," she said. "Let's go."

"Where are we?" I asked.

"I hope you are good at keeping secrets; I kind of have the opinion you will be," she said as she took out the basket of food and her bag and locked the car. "Follow me."

We began walking through some trees before Piper climbed up a steep, rough hill. It was quite wild and there were brambles everywhere. When she reached the top she stopped and looked around cautiously. We had come to some barbed wire and ahead was a field of long grass. "Look over there," she said grinning and pointing at some castle ruins. "Fancy visiting our own private castle for lunch?" She parted the wire carefully, so I could climb through. "Be careful," she said as I gingerly put my leg through the gap. Once I was on the other side she passed me the basket and bags then I parted the wire, so she could follow. "Now, you might have guessed we shouldn't really be here as this castle hasn't been open to the public for years, but I think it's a very special place and should be enjoyed, so I sometimes come here alone to draw. You are the first person I have shared this with and I'm counting on you to keep it as our secret – are you up for that?"

My eyes widened with excitement and I found myself whisper back, "Yes." Piper wanted us to run across the field and keep low, just in case anyone else could see us entering the site unlawfully, although the place did look completely deserted. By the time we reached the walls of the castle we were breathing very heavily and both collapsed in a heap on the grass laughing.

"Just one more bit then we'll be safe inside." Piper's eyes sparkled with delight as she moved along the wall until she came to a gap and disappeared inside the castle. I followed closely, passed her our things and also entered the cool cavity.

Behind the wall there were shafts of sunlight coming through from above warming up the stone. Most of the roof was missing, and the internal walls were just made up of broken sections. Grass was sporadically growing on the ground and there were several points where you could see straight through to the field outside. I could see why Piper liked it there. It was special, and with no one around it felt like it just belonged to us.

"I'm starving, let's have our picnic first," Piper said as she placed a rug on the ground and started to empty the basket of goodies. Endless little tubs and packets seemed to come out of the basket until the rug was almost covered. "Now, dig in," she said as she handed me a plate.

"This looks amazing!" I said as I tentatively took some carrot sticks and put them on my plate. Piper started helping herself and eating and talking, and was just so relaxed I soon felt comfortable enough to join in. We ate nearly everything – all in a random order – a bit of cake, then a sandwich and a tomato. It reminded me of being at a children's birthday party. It was nothing like a picnic with Ava; she wouldn't let us have anything sweet until we had eaten all the savoury things first. In between eating, Piper and I talked. It felt like we had known each other for years as we chatted and laughed together. I wondered if this was what having a proper older sister would be like, after all Piper could only have been seven or eight years older than me. As we talked more I began to notice that every time she mentioned her boyfriend, Luke, a pained look came over her face. Eventually, I decided to quiz her about him.

"We met two years ago now. He works in the school, but you won't know him as he's not a teacher. He's strictly admin; he has to deal with admissions and marketing; he helped me to get the job there. At first, I was so grateful; it's such a great place to work, but now I think it was just so he could keep a close eye on me. He's become so possessive; if any of the other staff talk to me then later on in the evening he says I was leading them on. If I ever tried to leave then that would be the end of my career. He would spread some vicious rumour about me, so I couldn't get a reference for another post. It's got to the stage now that even my family don't believe me, and my dad just thinks I should be thankful I have someone who cares so much about me." She began to cry a little. "I'm trapped. I don't know how to escape. I even had to come up with some story about visiting my aunt just to get away today."

She looked earnestly over at me then lay back on the ground in the dappled sunshine and closed her eyes. I didn't know how to respond, so I just sat in silence. Eventually she fell asleep.

I felt so sorry for Piper. Despite how our friendship had grown over the recent months, I had no idea until now what she was having to endure. She seemed like a lovely person and always so upbeat. I couldn't understand why anyone would want to cause her so much pain. After listening to her I was unable to relax, so I decided to explore the castle. I climbed up a stone staircase; it had the wall on one side but nothing on the other and by the time I reached the top and looked down I was quite high up.

The castle was too crumbled to work out where the rooms should be and there were only patches of wooden flooring and beams. Light flooded in from above and I could see straight up into the blue sky. There was a hole in the wall next to me, probably where a window would have been, so I climbed up and swung one leg over, straddling the wall and looked out across the field. I saw a deer in the far expanse, oblivious to me watching. It looked so peaceful, just munching on the grass, and keeping an eye out for danger. From up here I could see for miles; just fields and woodland all the way to the horizon.

I looked down at Piper sleeping on the ground beneath the steps. I wondered if I could trust her with my secrets; after all she had opened up to me. Not yet, I decided. I did however need to think of a plan so that Ava didn't root through my bag later. I absolutely couldn't risk her finding the gun. If she found out it would all have to come out: Bill's deal with Dave about the container, Dave's subsequent disappearance, the men that came to the garage, Troy's death and Bernie's suicide; it was all linked. In fact now I thought about it, the only good thing that had come out of the whole saga was that by stealing the gun it had helped me escape from my would-be kidnappers.

I was wearing shorts and a T-shirt so wouldn't be able to hide it on me anywhere. I looked over to check Piper was still asleep. I crept back down the stone staircase, took my jumper and laid it on the ground. I quietly took the gun from my rucksack and placed it inside the jumper, then wrapped the material around it and used the arms of the jumper to tie a knot over the whole thing. I gently placed it at the bottom of the picnic basket, then put the empty food containers and packets on top until it was completely hidden. I knew Piper would notice my jumper there when she got home but hoped she wouldn't think to unravel it. I hated the idea of putting her in the precarious position of discovering a firearm but ultimately, it was a risk I was going to have to take to avoid Ava finding me out first. Just then Piper made a few sleepy noises and sat up stretching.

"Oh, I must have dropped off for a minute. Sorry. Ah, you have cleared up, great. We'd better do a bit of drawing I suppose before it gets late. Come on, bring your sketchbook; let's find a good spot."

She picked up the blanket and shook it down, folding it up and putting it on top of the basket, wedging in everything underneath. That was it. My gun was going home to Piper's. I desperately hoped it would be safe.

We spent a couple of hours drawing before heading back to the car and starting the long journey back home. We didn't stop this time but Piper still chatted most of the way. I dropped into conversation a few hints on how difficult my own family life was, trying to lay some foundations for Piper to think about if she found my gun later that evening, desperately hoping she wouldn't be so scared she would take it straight to the police.

As we neared my house she said that perhaps I could say we just went to a spot in the New Forest for the day; you wouldn't know the difference from my drawings anyway. I agreed to keep her secret.

Ava met us on the drive. "Thank you so much, Miss Avery. See you at parents' evening next term," she said as she linked my arm to walk me inside. The inquisition was coming I could tell. As soon as we were in the hall she unlinked my arm and asked me to empty my bag under the pretence of seeing my drawings. I did as instructed, safe in the knowledge that she would find nothing of interest. I overenthusiastically talked about what a great teacher Miss Avery was as I emptied out my things and showed Ava my sketches. She tried to hide her disappointment at not finding anything incriminating, but she did want to know where my jumper was. I said I must have left it in the car and would check next time I saw Miss Avery. Once the interrogation was over, I went up to my room. All that I could think about now was what Piper would do if she discovered my secret: would she keep it or was my life about to explode?

CHAPTER 11

Bill had his appointment in Harley Street as planned and at the weekend I asked Ava what the new doctor had reported. She said they had taken some full body scans and X-rays, but would have to wait a week for the results. I would be back at school by then which I wasn't particularly looking forward to. I hadn't heard anything from Piper since our trip out, and I was dreading seeing her at school. However, I'd convinced myself that if she was going to tell Bill and Ava – or worse, the police – she would have done so by now. I knew I didn't have a choice but to hide the gun; nonetheless, I really missed not having it with me for protection.

The first day back at school was like one of those very late summer days. The sun was shining more than it had throughout August yet there was ever such a slight chill in the air, so you had the feeling autumn was just around the corner. Every year group had been allocated a new classroom, which had pre-selected name tags on each desk, so no one could choose where to sit. I had been put next to Layla; all I knew about her was that her dad was in charge at the local police station, and she was a bit of a goody-goody. We hadn't really decided if we liked or disliked each other in the previous year, and as she didn't have many friends either, I thought I should make an effort. There was a real buzz in the classroom as everyone was busy talking about their holidays and catching up, and I was desperate to tell someone about my first kiss.

"Did you have a good holiday?" I offered.

"Not really. I spent most evenings babysitting for my brother while my parents went out to work dos and parties. I did get lots of reading done though so I should be ready for the new English syllabus," Layla replied. She didn't offer any follow-up questions for me, so I thought it best to save my gossip for another time.

We were given our new timetables. I scanned the first day – the last lesson was art with Miss Avery. I was going to have to wait all day to face her. When it finally came round she had set up a still life for the class to draw and got us all working quietly. She moved around the room as usual looking at everyone's work and giving them suggestions, but she didn't come over to me.

In fact, it wasn't until after the last bell had rung that she looked at me at all. "Stay behind a moment please, Catherine; I'd like to see you about something."

Once all the other students had left the room she went to her belongings hanging on the back of her chair and took out a plastic bag with something in it. She threw it at me to catch.

"You left your jumper in my car, so I gave it a wash for you," she said calmly. I opened the bag and there at the bottom, neatly folded, was my jumper. I took it out of the bag; there was nothing else there. I looked up at Miss

Avery blankly. "You should be more careful with your possessions; you wouldn't want to lose anything and that is such a lovely jumper," she continued before putting on her coat and leaving the room.

I was left in the empty classroom alone. I wanted to shout after her *'what have you done with my gun?'* But I couldn't move. How could I ask her now? My surprise began to be replaced with anger. It was my gun, not hers to keep. Why hadn't she given it back or even said anything about it? Was she keeping it to protect me…or herself? I stuffed the jumper angrily into my bag and went to collect my things from the locker room so I could go home. Ava would be waiting outside by now and would have all sorts of questions about my first day.

When I got in the car Ava gave me a brief look and then just started the journey home. After about ten minutes the silence began to make me feel nervous; I must have done something bad. Maybe Miss Avery had spoken to her after all? It wasn't like Ava to bottle things up though. If I was in trouble she would be screaming at me by now. Eventually I plucked up enough courage to ask her.

"Had a good day?"

The sound of my voice seemed to make Ava jump. "Oh, yes it was fine. Sorry I was miles away. Dr Bedson's secretary called and asked us to go and see them tomorrow. She wouldn't give me any inkling why the sudden rush to see Bill; we had an appointment booked for Friday but that's not soon enough apparently." Her voice faded away as she went back into deep thought.

"Sounds like it will be good news," I ventured. I could sense Ava was nervous; she was never this quiet.

We finished the journey home in silence.

Later that evening I heard Bill on the phone: he was giving instructions to Richard about a meeting he would have to take his place for the next day. "You have been doing really well, Richard. I think that other business has blown over now. I caught up with Bob earlier and he said the police have finished their enquiries and don't have any leads on the culprits so his insurance claim should go through now. We may never know where that car ended up; it was a professional job, so they will have covered their tracks well. Anyway, I'm sure you can handle this meeting tomorrow without me. Just make sure Miles doesn't bully you into any more than five per cent discount, and even then he needs to commit to a multiple purchase – got it?"

I was glad to hear Richard was being given more responsibility. The other traders would soon trust him again thanks to Bill, and he could get his life back on track. Now and again I thought about Billie-Joe, and where he was now; I wondered if we would ever see him again. Hopefully not.

For once, I was keen to get in the car with Ava after school the next day to hear what the doctor had said. I had been worrying about Bill, watching him in pain all the time. I had detected he had started to avoid certain activities and was noticeably walking in discomfort.

"What happened with the new doctor?" I asked Ava straight away.

"Well…they have discovered it's not MS at all. The scans have detected a piece of bone growing through the spine very high up in the back. It's very unusual and would have been easy to miss as the pain has always been in the legs so Patrick never thought to investigate that high up the spine. Anyway they want to operate immediately as it's close to growing right through the spine and causing very serious damage. They say that after the operation all the pain will go and he can get back to a completely normal life," Ava reported.

"Oh, so his best friend has been wrong for all these years?" I said with some anger.

"Well, as I said it is a very unusual thing to happen. It's thanks to new technology and a different way of looking at things that has come up with these results. Who can say now that if they had seen this to start with things would have been different? Patrick is coming over later to see us; we haven't told him yet, so don't say anything when you see him."

"When are they going to do the operation?" I asked her.

"Next week," Ava snapped.

"How long will it take?"

"I don't know. He will need plenty of rest for a few weeks but after that he should be completely better."

I thought about this news. I couldn't help but blame Patrick. He was drunk half the time; it's no wonder he missed something so important.

"You should sue Patrick," I said.

"It is what it is now. It won't help to have someone to blame. I'm just pleased they found it now and can sort it out, and Bill can lead a normal life," Ava replied. I wondered why she was being so protective over Patrick; after all she was the one who pushed for a second opinion.

When we got home, Bill was in his study. He hadn't gone back to work after the appointment, but was still making deals over the phone.

"Pop a cup of tea down to him while I start the dinner," Ava asked me.

I waited while she made two cups of tea then carried one to the study. As I started down the long corridor I could hear Bill's voice; he was on the phone to Jane. I could always tell from the tone of his voice. Even from Germany, Jane was still his favourite; maybe it was because she was such a long way away, and he couldn't see all her bad behaviour that he had built up this image of an angel. He talked to her in such a gentle, loving way, *'Oh that's wonderful, darling; oh you are so clever.'* It made me want to puke. I burst in with the tea without knocking. Immediately he stopped talking and turned red. "Thanks, just put it there." He pointed at the corner of the desk and put his hand over the phone and waited patiently for me to leave. "Close the door on your way out."

I left but Bill knew I would still be in earshot and shortly after, he ended the call.

As I walked back up the corridor to the hall, I saw a car pull in. It was Patrick. I decided it was better not to see him. I wasn't sure I could bottle up what I knew and pretend everything was normal, so I darted upstairs and hid out of sight. Ava could let him in. He rang the bell, then opened the door anyway calling out hello. Ava appeared out of nowhere to greet him. She glanced down the corridor towards the study to check Bill's whereabouts then embraced Patrick briefly before looking around again. She whispered something in his ear then took his hand and led him down to the study and out of my sight. I heard Bill greeting his friend before Ava reappeared, presumably sent to fetch some drinks. I went to my room. It was up to Bill to decide what to say to Patrick; I didn't care anymore.

The day of the operation soon came around. Ava had arranged for me to go home after school with Layla – only because she knew her mother from aerobics. She hadn't actually asked me first. Layla looked really pleased to have an after school visitor and hoped it wasn't just a one-off. I hadn't told anyone about Bill's new diagnosis but when I saw Layla she asked why I was going over to her house.

"My dad's having an operation on his back today. My mum will be stuck at the hospital and isn't sure how long they will take," I said casually.

"Oh, I hope he's all right," Layla said.

"Yes, he will be fine; better than ever apparently."

"Well, I've got a bit of gossip that will take your mind off it," Layla said with a little grin. She was never naughty, so I didn't expect too much. "You have to promise not to tell anyone or I'll get in big trouble. You know my dad is a police inspector? Well, I heard him telling Mum about a shooting! Imagine that – a shooting here in our little town." Layla had the cheekiest face as she told me her secret news.

My interest perked up. "Who?" I asked Layla.

"I don't know; it was just last night and I didn't hear the beginning of the conversation, but we could try to find out more later when you come over."

Layla telling me this news did surprise me; she must be keener for a friend than I thought to spill the beans on her dad. Now I was quite looking forward to going round later and finding out more.

I stayed close and friendly to Layla all day so she would be more likely to spy on her dad later. By the end of the day I had her eating out the palm of my hand. It was her mum who picked us up. She was like one of the mums in a TV commercial: perfectly dressed and bubbly and keen for us to sample the cakes she had been baking at home all day.

"I hope you like lasagne. I've put extra cheese on the top, and made a fresh salad and home-made garlic bread to go with it," she gleamed. "Dinner will be at six when George comes in from work."

"Sounds wonderful," I smiled back, actually thinking it really did sound good and looking forward to meeting Layla's dad and seeing if he had any news on the shooting.

Their house was immaculate; it was like a show home. Everything had its place and was sparklingly clean. We went into the kitchen first where the table was already set with tea and cake. Layla's mum served us a slice each and then left us alone, so she could continue to work in the garden.

I couldn't wait to start our hunt for more information on the killing. "Where's your dad's study?" I asked Layla.

"It's just down the corridor, but I don't think we should go in there…he would be so cross if he found out."

"He's not here and your mum's outside – how will he find out? Come on, we've got to find out more on this shooting; let's go."

I knew she didn't want to let me down, she was so enthusiastic to make a friend, so Layla stood up and nervously led me to the study. Once inside I peeped through the window and spotted her mum bent over some rose bush in the garden.

"You keep an eye on your mum; I'll have a scan through these papers," I whispered.

The desk was as tidy as the rest of the house. On top were neat piles of brown folders, all with a title written on a sticky label on the front. I flicked down the pile. Burglary: Martinstown, Theft: O'Brien, Traffic Accident: Taylor; the pile went on. As well as the name they were all dated. None of the dates were recent and after carefully scanning all the piles of files there was nothing relating to a shooting.

"Where were your parents when you heard them talking about it?" I asked Layla.

"They were in here. I was meant to be in bed, but I forgot to take a cup of water upstairs and I was thirsty, so I crept down to the kitchen. I thought they would just be in the lounge watching TV, but then I heard them talking in here. It's unusual for my dad to be working so late, so I listened for a moment. I just heard the end of him saying there had been a shooting and he had to go out. I darted back upstairs then and Dad went out the house."

"If he had only just got the news then perhaps there wouldn't be a file yet." I went around and sat down at the desk. There was a telephone and next to it a notepad. I opened the pad; the page was blank, and there were a few shreds where the previous page had been torn out. I ran my finger over the paper and could feel bumps where the preceding page had made an imprint of words. I ripped the page out and closed the pad. "Let's go up to your bedroom and use a pencil to see what was written on the previous page. Maybe he got the news over the phone and made some notes which he took with him last night."

We carefully left the room making sure to leave everything exactly as it was and went straight upstairs. I could tell that although Layla was relieved to be out the study she was getting really excited at the adventure I was taking her on.

"Get a soft pencil," I instructed her.

She gave me one and I grabbed a book to lean on and lay down on the floor with the pencil on its side and began delicately shading the page until words began to appear as if by magic. Layla lay down beside me and read out the words as they materialised:

"Gunshot heard at 34 Hay Lane at 8:34pm… Neighbour called 999 … Firearms unit found white male dead on arrival … Female found uninjured next to victim … suspected weapon located and disarmed … Address registered to Miss Piper Avery."

I had coloured the whole page in and now the words were like floating white shapes under a dirty grey sea. Layla and I sat up abruptly and looked at each other absolutely stunned, our eyes like saucers. I took in a large gulp of air and let out the statement:

"Miss Avery has killed her boyfriend."

Layla jumped to her defence, "You don't know that. We don't have all the facts, and Dad always says you need all the facts before you can make a judgement."

I already knew the facts though. What has she done? I remembered our picnic and her telling me how horrible he was – abusive even, but to kill him…oh no…I took in another slug of air as the realisation hit me: she had used my gun.

CHAPTER 12

Layla's dad hadn't come back by dinner time so her mum let us eat on our own. Layla and I ate in silence, still stunned by our discovery. Almost the second we had finished Ava appeared to pick me up. I had been so busy thinking about Miss Avery that I had forgotten all about Bill and the operation. I politely said my thank-yous to Layla's mum and awkwardly told Layla I would see her at school the next day. We nervously looked at each other, not able to find the words in front of the adults before I got in the car with Ava.

"So how did it go?" I asked her.

In her usual matter-of-fact voice she replied, "All as planned. Apparently the bone had grown a little more than they had expected, but we should know more tomorrow when the anaesthetic has completely worn off."

"Right," was all I could answer. More waiting. At least the operation had gone well.

My thoughts went straight back to Piper and my gun. The image of her on the floor next to her dead boyfriend, blood all over the place appeared in my mind. She didn't even run away! Stupid woman. Now she would be questioned by the police and would have to tell them where she got the gun, and then everything that had happened would come out. If Bill had been home I might have confessed; despite his initial fury he would know what to do. What would he say? How could he sort this one out? I tried to imagine being him, hearing my account for the first time. He would say I needed a watertight story as to how I came to have a gun in my possession. It would have my fingerprints on it, so I can't deny ever seeing it. I could say I found it, when I was on the picnic with Piper and I slipped it in the basket so it was safe, assuming she would hand it in. Yes, that was plausible. I needed to divert attention away from Bill and the container. After all, Piper didn't know where I got it from, so she couldn't say otherwise. I felt better now I had a plan. We arrived home, and I went straight to my room letting Ava think I just needed an early night and I was tired after worrying all day about Bill.

At school the next day before registration, everyone was talking about the shooting. They were a day behind Layla and me though, as they were yet to hear it was at Miss Avery's house. Layla wasn't in yet which was unusual; she was never off sick. Mrs Markell, the head teacher, came into our classroom and announced there would be a special assembly this morning, and we should file quietly into the hall. The whole school was crammed in and it was like a beehive now with all the buzz of gossip. At the front on the stage the teachers were lined up as usual then I spotted someone at the side dressed in a smart police uniform, hat under one arm. Mrs Markell requested silence, and then all eyes were on her. She introduced

Police Commissioner George Blunt to the school then stepped back so he could speak. It was Layla's dad.

"Good morning, children. I need to inform you that there was an incident on Wednesday at Miss Avery's home. I can't go into details, but I want anyone who has any information about Miss Avery's behaviour lately to stay behind and tell me. Even if it's just a trivial thing, it might help us with our enquiries so please do think carefully."

The low hum began again as everyone started hushed whispers of conspiracy theories. Mrs Markell clapped her hands. "Back to class now, everyone, unless you have something to say to the Commissioner."

Now I had a dilemma. If I told them about Piper's abusive boyfriend it could help her case, but might also draw attention to myself. I decided to start a rumour. Mary-Jane was the best person to tell; it would be all round the school by lunchtime, and no one would know how it started. I placed myself next to her on the way out of the hall, and amidst all the other gossiping and chatter slipped in, so she could hear, "It's shocking news, isn't it? Do you think Miss Avery is connected to the shooting? Remember how she always went on in our lessons about her abusive boyfriend? I hope she got rid of him." Then I ducked out of the way and into the crowd. That would have to do. I just had to wait to see how many people Mary-Jane told, and hope it somehow got back to the Commissioner.

How right I was: by lunch break my classmates were asking me if I knew about Miss Avery's abusive boyfriend. Everyone knew I was good at art and had teased me on many occasions about being the teacher's pet. I just agreed and suggested the class captain should talk to the Head about it. There, that was the best I could do. Now all I had to hope was that Piper hadn't let on where she got the gun. The further through the day I got the more confident I began to feel that she hadn't said anything; the police would have come to question me by now, surely?

Ava was waiting for me in the car. For once, it was going to be me giving her some dramatic news, but when I got in the car her face was swollen with the after-effects of tears. Her eyes were puffy and the end of her pointy nose red. She gave me a quick smile then began driving.

"What?" I asked nervously.

"I've just come from the hospital. The head consultant, Doctor Burns, has just finished assessing Bill. He explained that the operation was more difficult than they had anticipated, and they ... they ... don't expect he will be able to walk ever again." The last words tailed off as she began sobbing quietly again, tears flowing down her cheeks which she kept brushing away as she tried to concentrate on the road. We sat in silence for a moment while I digested this information.

Eventually, I asked the most obvious question, "Why do they think he won't walk again?" Ava tried to compose herself, and cleared her throat and shook her head briskly as if to tell herself that was quite enough of that emotion in my presence.

"Because they had to pretty much cut right through his spine to remove the growth. He has no feeling in his legs now and although it is early days, they think he will be paralysed for the rest of his life."

One feeling after another came across me like a rollercoaster. First, the anger. This was all Patrick's fault. If he hadn't been drunk the whole time and done his job properly Bill would never have needed this operation. Next came the thought of Bill in a wheelchair – how could he manage in our home? How would he get upstairs? How would he drive to work? He was such a tall, strong figure, I simply couldn't imagine him unable to move and it just didn't fit. Finally, the shock took me over. It felt like I was trapped in a tarpaulin tent that had collapsed, unable to move or see, and weighed down with no way out.

We arrived home. Ava looked over at me before getting out. She composed herself and said, "Come on, it will all be all right. It's just going to take some organising and getting used to. Let's go in and start the dinner."

"Does Shawn know?" I asked her. Shawn went to a different school and had a taxi service drive him home every day. He would already be inside.

"Yes, Shawn didn't go into school today. He came to the hospital with me and stayed behind with Bill so I could pick you up. I'll have to pop back to the hospital after dinner to collect him."

She gave my leg a little squeeze before jumping out and heading into the house. I remained in the car dumbfounded. Shawn had gone to the hospital? Why had I been sent to school and not him? Did she not realise how upsetting this news would be? What if I wanted to go to the hospital? I felt so shut out and alone. I got out the car and stormed inside ready to demand answers from Ava, but as I reached the kitchen doorway I heard she was on the phone already. She waved her hands at me as if to suggest I leave the room, so she could have privacy. This dismissal just made my blood boil and I ran up to my room and slammed the door, fell face first onto my bed and began deeply sobbing.

Half an hour later Ava called up to say dinner was in the oven and she was just going to collect Shawn while it cooked, giving me instructions to set the table. I heard the front door slam, signifying she had left without waiting for an answer.

When they returned, I was waiting at the table ready for battle, but on seeing Ava and Shawn's sombre faces quickly realised now was not the time for recrimination. This was too serious. How had I let jealousy get a hold of my head? I wondered. Now was the time to pull together, for Bill's sake. Ava explained how, over the next few weeks, there would be mobility specialists assessing how to adapt the house for wheelchair use. They were going to change the study into a bedroom temporarily as it was downstairs and install ramps outside the front door and wherever there were little steps inside. They wouldn't install a chairlift at this stage, but it would be something to consider later.

The impact this was going to have on our lives slowly began to dawn on me.

"When will he be able to come home?" I asked.

"Not for some time while he properly gets over the operation. You can come and visit tomorrow if you like. I think one day off school won't hurt."

"Actually, I'd rather wait until the weekend. I don't want to miss any lessons at the moment." I wasn't feeling ready to see Bill in that state just yet, and I needed to see Layla urgently and find out any updates about Piper.

As it turned out, I wasn't the only one keen to speak to Layla. When I arrived in the classroom there was a swarm of students around her; she loved the attention, I could tell. Questions were being fired at her to try to find out any snippets of information. Layla was acting quite coy and was giving nothing away, then the bell went and we had to take our seats.

"How's your dad?" she asked me.

"The doctors have paralysed him," I replied quite bluntly, looking away as water began to fill my eyes.

"Oh that's terrible," said Layla, shocked at my statement whilst looking at me as though she really did care.

"Yes it is. I'm sorry but I'd rather not talk about it. Tell me what you know about Miss Avery."

"Oh well, my dad didn't come home until really late again, but my mum asked me if I knew anything about Miss Avery's boyfriend being abusive. Apparently someone told my dad yesterday that she used to tell us that in class. I don't remember her saying that, do you?"

"Yes, I think she did say that a couple of times. I remember seeing some bruises on her when she rolled her sleeves up to wash the palettes," I lied.

"Well I don't blame her then; what a bastard. I overheard Dad say that she has admitted to shooting her boyfriend, but insists she found the gun in his stuff. If she can't prove it was her boyfriend's weapon then she must have acquired it illegally; therefore she intended to use it to kill him and it was premeditated. That is murder and she will never be free again."

"What if it was his gun though?"

"Well, the fact remains she still shot him but if it was self-defence then it's manslaughter, and she would get between five and ten years in prison," Layla replied with an air of confidence as if she was a legal adviser.

A huge wave of guilt washed over me. If Piper hadn't said where she got the gun by now then she might keep it secret forever. Maybe it wouldn't help the investigation to know where it came from. It had been her choice to kill him and end her life of misery. But what would help is if they could link the gun to her boyfriend, Luke. She had told me he worked in the admin part of the school and those offices were just past the staffroom. Students were only allowed in there to hand in doctors' notes. What if I could plant some evidence in there? I remembered the white box of bullets. It was still wrapped up in my clothes in the bottom drawer at home in my bedroom. I'd left it there after I'd loaded the gun not knowing quite what to do with it. I needed to hide it in Luke's office. I would have to do it tomorrow and hope the police hadn't already searched there by then.

As the day dragged on the gossip about Miss Avery was rife; I heard bits of conversation about how her boyfriend used to beat her up and forbid her from seeing friends. Even the other teachers seemed totally obsessed with it. The fact was that although she had always seemed a bit of a loner, most people didn't actually know her very well and were now feeling guilty at not noticing the signs. Overnight she had become a martyr and no one had a bad word to say about her. Her boyfriend Luke wasn't mentioned; it was like he didn't exist. It was sad that they hadn't been friendlier and a bit more supportive when she was around so this whole awful situation hadn't needed to happen at all.

I was dreading going home. I didn't want to hear any more bad news about Bill, and I had a strong suspicion there would be more to come.

Ava picked me up as usual. Although she had spent most of the day in the hospital, there was no more news, and we spent most of the journey in silence. Once home I went to the kitchen to make some tea while she began making phone calls to various business associates of Bill. He had written a long list of jobs for her to do, starting with contacting Richard in the garage. Even with everything that had happened, and from his hospital bed, Bill couldn't let go of the business. Ava read out the information to Richard in a monotone voice. She didn't know what it all meant. Deliveries, stock checks and meetings, the list went on until she finally said Bill had requested a daily update from Richard, so she would call him again tomorrow. Next it was Fat Jack's turn.

"Hello, Jack…yes, yes thank you, I heard you were poorly too?…Ah well, I'm sure it will pass. Listen, Bill has asked me to let you know he needs to close down the ABC Cars business, and have the cash now. He said you would know what he meant; can you arrange that?"

There was a long silence while I assume Jack answered then Ava replied in a slightly high-pitched voice, "Why not? Bill isn't going to be available for a meeting for some time, and he said it was just sitting there waiting for a rainy day. Well it's more than raining now; it's a full-blown bloody storm and we need that money, Jack, understand?...Well I don't understand why you can't just deal with me; I am his wife!" There was another long silence then Ava quietly put the phone down. I guessed Jack wasn't going to simply let Ava access the money she needed. She wasn't up for dealing with all this. Bill hadn't involved her in any of the business affairs for so many years and she had no idea how to cope without him. She pulled herself together enough to make a couple more calls: one to Digger informing him of Bill's condition, and one to a care home setting up a meeting to assess the Chatter Nan for re-homing, before disappearing upstairs with a migraine.

I went up to my room and located the white box and put it in my school bag. Now all I had to work out was how to get it into position. I had been in the admin area a couple of times before to give a sick note in. It was located just past the staffroom. You had to go through a fire door, and into an open-plan area where there was a large desk in the middle where the secretary sat, then behind her were the offices. I guessed one of them was Luke's. I thought about several options: handing in a sick note then pretending to be sick, setting off the fire alarm, waiting until lunch break and hoping the admin staff all went out. But none of these would get me into his office unseen. Eventually I decided to forge a sick note as a back-up, and wait until the secretary was doing her rounds collecting the registers before slipping out to Luke's office and praying no one saw me.

On the way to school the next day I was exhausted. I didn't sleep all night worrying about my task. I knew I would only have a very small window of opportunity when the secretary would be out of her office, and I had to get this right. Five minutes before the end of registration I excused myself from the classroom with the little white box and my forged note stuffed down my jumper. I ran down to the toilets nearest to the staffroom and waited for the secretary to leave her post. Within seconds, I heard her heels click past. I opened the door a crack to check it was her; it was. Right, I had about ten minutes before she would be back from her rounds. I crept past the staffroom, and down to the fire door leading to the admin area. I slid through the smallest of gaps and into the open-plan office.

There was the secretary's desk, and behind that, half-glazed doors with name tags on them. I darted to the first one; I could see someone was sitting at the desk, so I crawled under the window and stopped before the next door. I peeped through the glass but couldn't see anyone inside. I looked at the name tag: Peter Baines. Not this one either then. I went to the third door. This one had Luke Roberts written on it. I didn't know his surname but this room was empty as well and there was only one more office left. I was just wondering if I should check the last one just in case there were two Lukes when I saw the door handle move down on the last office. Someone was coming out. I ducked inside Luke Roberts's office quickly. The shadow of a woman walked past the window. They hadn't noticed me; phew! This must be the right room; now, where to place the box? I went behind the desk.

There were a few piles of papers and a pot of pens, and behind his computer a photo of Piper. I told myself not to faff but just stuff it somewhere and get out. I opened a desk drawer. It was incredibly neat, with folders piled up, I couldn't just throw it in there. I opened the bottom one. This had more of an assortment of bits in it: paper clips, rubbers, pens, etc. I put the little white box at the back giving it a last wipe to remove my fingerprints – not that I really thought that would matter now. I went to the door and checked through the glass: the coast looked clear. I slipped out and had just reached the secretary's desk when the fire door opened and Mrs Markell walked in with two police officers.

"What are you doing in here?" she asked me with that usual air of authority.

I quickly whipped my sick note out: "I was just waiting to give this to the secretary."

"Just leave it on the desk and get to class quickly; there's no need to hand it in personally."

I could tell from her tone that if she hadn't had company to deal with I would have been in a lot more trouble. I placed the screwed up note on the desk, rushed past her and the officers and out into the safety of the corridor. I was sweating; that was too close and I had been within seconds of being caught. I hoped that the sight of the police officers meant that they hadn't yet searched Luke's office or at least were going in for another look and would discover the evidence Piper needed. I rushed back to class; all I could do now was wait.

CHAPTER 13

Before I knew it, Saturday came around, and it was time to visit Bill. I didn't want to go but knew I couldn't avoid it any longer. Ava had packed a little picnic basket for us and had included Bill's favourite foods. The three of us departed as if heading off for a fun day out. Except it wasn't fun. I travelled in the back of the car, Shawn in front. None of us spoke all the way. When we reached the hospital, Ava put four hours' worth of parking on the car before leading the way to Bill's ward.

I had only been in a hospital once before, and that was when I was very small, so it felt very strange to be inside such a place. Long corridors with polished floors seemed to penetrate in every direction like a maze. Signs directed visitors towards closed doors which in turn led to more corridors and departments. Doctors and nurses walked around at speed in their pale uniforms and squeaky shoes with vacant expressions and a clear 'Do Not Disturb' notice written across their faces. Ava led us through the building. We went up three floors in a lift and seemed to walk for at least ten minutes before entering the Orthopaedic Ward. She headed straight to Reception and chatted with a few nurses as if they had been friends for years.

By the time I started paying attention, a particularly jolly member of the team was saying, "Bill already has a visitor with him this morning."

"Oh, who is that?" replied Ava, annoyed at not having been informed before her arrival.

"His son," said the nurse.

Ava's usual upbeat persona noticeably crumbled. She quickly shook herself down and replied with a little laugh, "Of course, I had completely forgotten that Billie-Joe was coming in today." It was obvious to the rest of us she didn't know though. We hadn't seen or heard from him for months now. I had played the scene in my head so many times of when I next saw him, and how I would smash his head in for what he had done. Now suddenly, the prospect of seeing him in a few seconds with Bill in the room as well, in his condition, and with Ava and Shawn there too knowing nothing of the history completely threw me. I felt like my head would burst; I wished I could run down all those endless corridors and into oblivion.

"Come on." Ava was nudging me forward, pushing me in front of her as if I was a shield. I opened the door and stepped into the room. Bill was there lying in the bed in his pyjamas, Billie-Joe and Digger sitting at the other side of the bed. I looked at Bill first; his legs were under the sheets as normal. I don't know why I thought they wouldn't be there but it was weird seeing the shape of them under the covers while thinking they were of no use any more. He looked weak and pale; a tube was taped to his arm which led up to a drip. Next to the bed were a clear jug, plastic cup and box of tissues. Nothing personal. Over on the other side of the room was his suitcase and toiletry bag. They only ever came out when we were going on holiday, I thought.

Bill must have seen my frightened expression taking in the room. "How was school this week?" he asked. *'How was school?'* I repeated to myself, completely stunned at such a stupid question. Still, I couldn't answer; I just stood there gaping. "Try not to worry; I'll soon be home and learning to walk again," he said. I turned sharply to look at him along with everyone else.

Ava quickly pushed past me and put the basket on the table that was hovering over the bed. "Just look what we have brought! Oh, hello, Billie-Joe – where have you been hiding? We weren't sure when you'd turn up. I assume you have been in touch with Digger then?" She cast an accusing look at Digger before carrying on, "We have Stilton in here and some crackers, some chocolate ginger and plenty of sandwiches for everyone." She emptied out the contents of the basket onto the little table as if we were about to have a children's party. There were even paper plates which she duly handed round. The atmosphere was awful. No one knew what to say and eating was definitely not on anyone's mind. We all stood there with empty plates. I cast a look of pure hatred at Billie-Joe. If I had been alone with him, I would be yelling at him by now, I thought.

Eventually it was Bill who broke the silence: he was obviously trying to put on a brave face and cheer us all up. "I'll be able to order you all around a lot more anyway."

Only Shawn forced a smile at the joke. Then a nurse came in and said Bill could go home as soon as he was strong enough and the house had been adapted. Digger said he had to get back to work and signalled to Billie-Joe that he was ready to leave.

"I'll move back in tonight," announced Billie-Joe. "Don't worry, Dad; I'll run the business until you are ready."

Ava turned to look at him. "You will do no such thing! I wouldn't trust you to drive me home let alone be responsible for our livelihood," she blurted out. "Where have you been anyway? Do you think you can just turn up and take charge? Well, there's no need. Bill, tell him Richard is more than capable of handling things."

"What's Richard got to do with it? Is he working for you?" asked Billie-Joe.

It occurred to me he didn't know Bill had put Richard in charge. I wondered why Digger hadn't told him, then I realised – almost at the same time as Billie-Joe. He looked over at me knowing I had grassed him up to Bill, then slowly his stare moved across to Bill. His face turned red, and tears began to form in his eyes at the realisation that Bill knew he had stolen the Bugatti all along yet hadn't informed the police. Instead, he gave Richard a job when his name was dirt as a recompense for what his children had done. He fell to his knees at the side of the bed, head down on the mattress reaching up to grab Bill's hand, repeatedly whispering he was sorry.

Ava, completely oblivious to the real reason, said in her matter-of-fact voice, "Oh come on, Billie-Joe; we are all in shock but grow up and act your age. Digger, take him home please, we'll talk later."

After Digger and Billie-Joe had left, and we'd all managed to eat something, Shawn and I went out to the coffee machine leaving Ava and Bill alone for a while.

"What did Dad mean when he said he'd be learning to walk again?" Shawn asked me.

I'd also been wondering about this and whether Ava had told us the whole story.

Billie-Joe managed to avoid me for the next week: I was at school all day and he was out by the time I got home. Maybe it was just as well now he knew I had told Bill. My anger had subsided after watching him break down in the hospital and I secretly hoped that perhaps even regretted the whole business. Builders were busy adapting the house and converting the study to a bedroom. A new electric bed had been delivered and to make room the big old desk had been pushed up against the wall of cupboards, so they could no longer be opened. It all looked very temporary.

Ava was busy giving out instructions and making phone calls. She seemed to be in her element – a purpose for her at last. Bill needed her for the first time and she was completely focussed on preparing for his homecoming. Even on our school car journeys she didn't talk to me or tell me the latest gossip, her mind occupied with more planning. The only snippet of information she confided in me was the fact that the nursing home she had found for the Chatter Nan was an hour's drive away, so we wouldn't have to go very often. Good, I thought guiltily, although I wondered how Bill would visit her now.

It had been decided that for the first month, while Bill got accustomed to his new disability, he would hire a private nurse. She would be able to teach Ava how to best help Bill to wash and get dressed as well as use all the fancy new equipment. After several interviews, Ava had chosen a rather plain looking woman called Sue. I heard them agreeing a fee of £1000 per week. She would sleep in Jane's old room, and be on constant call twenty-four hours a day via a fancy new system that had been installed. Bill just had to press a button from beside his bed and a buzzer would sound in the kitchen as well as upstairs on the landing. For the duration of Sue's stay she would have to respond but after that it would be down to Ava.

The whole transformation was complete within a couple of months. Bill arrived by ambulance, already strapped in a wheelchair, so he was simply wheeled out the back doors and straight into the house. Ava, Shawn and I stood awkwardly on the porch acting like a welcoming committee, while Sue jumped into action taking charge of the wheelchair manoeuvring. He appeared quite upbeat as he greeted us all but I knew it was just an act.

"Take me down to my new quarters!" he joked as Sue pushed him into the hall. She duly wheeled him down the long corridor to the study. Ramps were now set up where the odd step had been. We all followed but at the entrance to Bill's new bedroom Ava turned to Shawn and me and whispered, "We don't want to crowd him, kids. Why don't you go and watch a film or something, and give Dad a moment to settle in?" She disappeared inside not waiting for an answer. Shawn and I turned away and slowly walked back up the corridor in silence to the sitting room. We slumped down in front of the TV. *Indiana Jones* was the afternoon movie, and was already halfway through, but we'd seen it before so it didn't matter. Neither of us could concentrate on it anyway. After about ten minutes Shawn randomly said, "I've got my driving test next week."

At that moment an overwhelming feeling that I'd been completely abandoned engulfed me. The next few years mapped out: Shawn off and away in his car; Billie-Joe disappearing again; Ava permanently working as a nurse for Bill, and me…where would I be?

We didn't see Bill again until dinner. He managed to wheel himself into the kitchen, then proceeded to make several movements backwards and forwards until he was facing the table. Sue hovered behind, making the odd grunt of encouragement as Bill did his best. Ava had made up a tray of food for Sue, so she could go and eat in the dining room. It must have been decided at some point that family dinners would exclude her services. Shawn and I sat in silence as Bill awkwardly held onto the table with one hand while attempting to cut and eat his food with the other, his entire focus was on trying to balance and eat at the same time. Ava tried to help by cutting up his food, but he quickly ushered her away.

"I can manage. I won't be like this for long anyway. My new physio arrives on Monday and she'll soon have me walking again."

We all looked blankly at him. The doctor had said he would never walk again; why did he keep insisting he would be fine?

I found it very odd in the beginning, seeing my tall, strong father always sitting. His strength and power seemed diminished just as a result of being physically lower than everyone else. Over the next few months his legs quickly lost their muscle and looked like sticks through the stretchy tracksuit bottoms he wore instead of his usual suit. He seemed to swiftly get the hang of the wheelchair, manoeuvring it around like a pro. Sue was always on hand in the background but apart from helping him to get ready in the morning and evening, he didn't really need her throughout the day and as soon as Ava learned the routine Sue was let go.

The physio came twice a week but all she seemed to do was move his legs around and give him some massage. There was never any suggestion of him walking or even standing. Family and friends came daily to visit. Bill stayed jovial with them, often joking around and saying he would soon be back on his feet. It became a bit of a weird pun in the end. Whenever he said it no one knew quite what to do or how to act. Maybe that was his way of staying in control.

One Sunday afternoon Richard came over with April. I hadn't seen them for ages. Bill had telephone conversations with Richard every day but not face-to-face meetings. April was pregnant – the IVF had finally worked – and they were expecting a baby girl. She was so grateful to Bill for giving Richard the job and the money, and believing in him when no one else did. Ava brought in some tea and cake and while we were all busy chatting, we didn't hear the front door open and Billie-Joe walk in.

"Hey, what's going on in here?" he said as he burst in. "Sounds like a party!" Then he saw who it was and immediately fell back inside his own shell and just stood like a statue in the middle of the room.

Richard stood up. "Hello, Billie-Joe, I haven't seen you for years!" The two men shook hands, Richard warmly putting his hand over Billie-Joe's to make a double clasp as he vigorously moved them up and down.

As they let go, Richard's gaze fell and for just a fraction of a second I saw his ever glowing smile falter, replaced with a whiteness like he'd had a shock, before resuming his jolly demeanour and sitting back down.

Billie-Joe composed himself before announcing, "Ah, I've just remembered I'm meant to be meeting Digger. Nice to see you guys again." And he smiled and waved, picking up a piece of cake before disappearing again leaving nothing but an intense aroma of his cheap Lynx aftershave hanging in the air.

I glanced at Bill who looked relieved Billie-Joe had left, before commenting, "Just look at the joys you two have to look forward to! Even after they have grown up they still need looking after, coming and going as they please like the place is a hotel!" Everyone laughed before resuming baby talk.

After several more months the visitors had dropped off; of course life goes on for everyone else. They all had their own problems to deal with and there wasn't anything anyone could do about Bill's situation. Ava had to give up all her various social activities, so that she was available in case Bill needed her, only popping out to do the shopping or the school pick up. Her appearance started to look neglected and her attire more on the practical side. She seemed to operate like a machine: get up, get Bill ready, get breakfast, get children to school, get shopping, get back, get lunch, get Bill ready for physio, get children from school, get dinner, get Bill to bed. Repeat. One day merged into another as this routine dominated her life. Shawn had passed his driving test and as predicted was out with his friends most of the time. I was left to my own devices.

I stayed friendly with Layla, mainly because I was still interested to hear any snippets of information about Piper, desperate to find out if my evidence had ever been found. She never had anything much to say until the day after the trial had started.

"So apparently Miss Avery's defence is going to try to prove it was manslaughter. They will need to demonstrate that Miss Avery was provoked into killing her boyfriend by a sudden loss of control. They are going to say she was suffering from a significantly altered state of mind after all the abuse she had suffered from him. She's still insisting she found the gun in Luke's stuff and hadn't planned to kill him, but just question him about it. Then, as their row escalated, she ended up using it herself in self-defence. Dad doesn't believe her story because although they found some other prints on the gun, they never recovered her boyfriend's from it."

I took in a sharp breath; I really needed to know if they ever found the white box but couldn't directly ask Layla so just casually said, "Did they find anything to suggest it was his gun?"

"I don't know; I only hear snippets of conversations about it. I know they couldn't find any evidence that she had acquired it herself. I guess all will be revealed in the trial."

I still felt deeply guilty, despite my best efforts to help. Why hadn't she told the police where the gun came from? If they had questioned me I would have admitted it; I still wondered if I should confess now. Was there still time to make a difference? They were my prints on the gun after all; it would prove I had handled the weapon. But then they would want to know where I got it from, and I couldn't tell them about that. Not now. "I'm going to be sick," I announced before running out of the classroom to the toilets and throwing up.

Shawn picked me up that day; Ava was relieved to hand over that job to him. Bill sorted him out with an old part-exchange Fiesta from the business that he needed to move on, in return for running a few errands to help out. I was one of them.

"What's up with you?" he said. "You look green."

"I'm not feeling well. Can we just go home?"

Shawn took the back route. There was a road quite near South Drive that was long and straight but had a dip in the middle. We had often cycled that way as you could go really fast down one side and get a good run up the hill after the dip. If Ava drove that way she went quite fast, and you got a butterfly feeling in your stomach – like a roller coaster as the car went through the dip.

"I know what will cheer you up," Shawn said, and he sped up as he got to the straight. There was no one coming the other way, so he accelerated even more. We went through the dip as usual giving us both a massive buzz but as we came back up, the front of the little car caught on the tarmac and sent the car into a spin. We circled a full 360 degrees; Shawn had his foot on the brake as we spun, his arms rigid on the steering wheel, his eyes wild with fear. As the car whirled I thought we would be smashed to pieces but it actually just came to an abrupt stop. Somehow the car was facing the right way, in the right position, still on the road. Smoke briefly surrounded us along with a stench of burning rubber, but we were absolutely fine. Shawn turned to face me, his look of fear changing to relief, and we both started giggling, then as reality set in of what had just happened and how lucky we were, it turned to laughter. We sat there until tears started falling. It was the first time I had let my emotions go in ages and it felt good just to get it all out. Laughter intermingled with crying, tears of joy and tears of fear; it all flowed out. Eventually Shawn calmed down enough to say, "Don't ever tell anyone about this," before starting the car, and finishing the journey home.

As we pulled in the drive, I ventured a question, "Shawn, if I promise not to say anything about the near-death experience you just put us through…will you do me a small favour?"

"Don't exaggerate! Near death! That's ridiculous; it was just a little spin," Shawn retorted. Then he thought for a moment. "What is this favour then?" He knew and I knew that if I retold our little experience in a slightly more animated way, Bill would probably take his car away and that would be the end of his freedom.

"Miss Avery's trial continues tomorrow. I want you to go along to watch and then tell me everything that happens. You can call into school sick first thing. Now you're in the sixth form they won't care, especially after everything you have been through this year; another day off won't hurt."

"Why do you want to know about the trial? I know she was your teacher but it's not like she was your friend."

"Actually we were quite friendly and I heard she is pleading manslaughter, and I just need to know what happens. We are all betting on it at school and I could make a lot of money if I knew which way the trial was going before everyone else."

"Well, I suppose I could. It might be interesting to watch. I'll only miss one lesson tomorrow anyway."

"Thanks. Listen really carefully to the evidence and let me know everything."

We went inside. I decided that if it looked awful for her tomorrow then I would hand myself in. Whatever I did the fact remained that she had still killed him, and if she could get away with manslaughter without my confession then that would be the best outcome.

CHAPTER 14

Of course, throughout the day I couldn't concentrate. I had told Ava I was staying late for an after-school club, and had arranged for Shawn to pick me up. She didn't object, pleased I was out of the way for a bit longer. At five o'clock I was waiting for Shawn, but it was another half an hour before he turned up. I jumped in his car. "So what happened?" I asked him urgently.

"Ah, it was great! I'm so pleased you got me to go. I think I might be a lawyer." He had a massive grin on his face clearly having enjoyed the day.

"But what happened?!" I barked again.

"Well, I found out that all that had happened on day one was the jury selection, so just as well I arrived on day two! First, Miss Avery had to state whether she was guilty or not guilty on the count of murder. She said in this tiny voice 'not guilty'. Then the Prosecution set out their case against her followed by her defence barrister making a statement on her behalf. He described how she had been acting in self-defence, terrified for her own life, and he would prove that was the case. By the time that had all happened it was lunchtime. After lunch witnesses were called. Not witnesses to the murder of course because there weren't any but police officers and specialists. One psychologist went on about Miss Avery's mental health being affected by the constant abuse from her partner. He said that years of constant abuse can build up and all be unleashed in a split second. In his professional opinion it was very unlikely Miss Avery had planned to kill Luke Roberts, as that would be too rational for her state of mind. During this final argument she just snapped and felt compelled to end it. The Prosecution did their best to dissolve that argument by suggesting that she was perfectly competent as she held down a very respectable teaching job and was completely professional throughout her position in the school. A few teachers backed up that theory as well. But the psychologist explained that it was perfectly normal for a victim to segregate their lives into compartments that they could deal with in completely different ways. He said that it was clear from her medical examination that she had suffered several serious physical injuries that had gone untreated, and of course there were the cuts and bruises she had sustained on the night in question. In his opinion she was the victim of severe mental and physical abuse. Then there were several further specialists who went over the severity of her injuries, which were pretty horrible."

"Was that it? Didn't they talk about the gun?"

"Well that was it for today. No one knows how long the whole trial will take but I asked the person next to me who was a law student, and he said he thought it wouldn't take too long, probably by the end of next week."

"Another week? Can you go again tomorrow?"

"No, I can't take a week off school as much as I might like to. I wish I'd chosen different A levels now as it was so interesting. I will go back in a couple of days and see where it's up to. I asked the law student, whose name is Carlos, to fill me in. We got on really well actually; it's quite useful to have someone explaining all the legal jargon."

When we pulled into the drive we saw there was an ambulance parked near the front door; we gave each other a worried look before rushing inside to find out what was going on. When we reached the porch, the paramedics were just coming out with a body on a stretcher. My mouth went dry and my heart felt like it had stopped beating altogether as horrific thoughts cascaded across my mind of it being Bill. Then as we came closer I saw it wasn't Bill on the stretcher at all but Fat Jack. Ava was following closely behind. Black mascara lines stained her face where she had been crying, and then behind her, Bill was wheeling himself along, a grim look on his face.

While Jack was loaded into the ambulance I noticed he wasn't moving at all, and the paramedics didn't seem to be working on him either. After strapping the stretcher in they closed the ambulance doors and both got in the front, leaving Jack alone in the back.

"What's happened?" Shawn and I said almost in unison as they drove away.

"Jack has had a heart attack," Ava said bluntly. Then seeing our concerned faces she quickly added, "Very sadly he died despite the paramedics' best efforts." Then she turned to Bill. "You need to call Sal and tell her what's happened straight away."

Bill didn't say a word but silently swivelled his wheelchair and disappeared off back into the hall and in the direction of his bedroom. Ava announced she was going upstairs to wash her face. Shawn and I were left standing there speechless, suddenly brought down after our previous enthusiastic journey and discussion. I can't admit I ever liked Jack, but he had been visiting Bill for as long as I could remember and had always been jovial and friendly to me.

"I think I'll go and start my homework. Thanks for today," I murmured to Shawn before quietly climbing the stairs to my room. Poor Jack; I didn't shed a tear but I did feel sad for his family. I loosely knew his wife Sal and his son Charles, although not very well as Jack tended to visit alone. Charles was also an accountant and worked in the firm with his dad although they were complete opposites – Charles was tall and smarmy, while Jack is more rotund and jolly. Well, he was.

Dinner was a sombre affair that evening. Ava, still looking teary, dished up a fish pie she had saved in the freezer for an occasion just like this when she didn't have time to cook. Bill sat in silence, his eyes hardly moving from his plate as he pushed the food around. Shawn and I couldn't talk about our day's events either to lighten the mood as they were top secret. Desperate for it to end, as soon as the last fork was put down I jumped up to collect the plates, and started the washing-up. Shawn did the same, and leaving the adults at the table we cleaned the plates together before excusing ourselves from the kitchen and disappearing off to our bedrooms. I really wanted to ask more details about what exactly had led to Jack's heart attack but felt it wasn't going to be met with answers just yet. Then my mind refocused on the other matter: the trial. There would be several more sleepless nights before I would know the outcome of that.

Shawn arranged to go back to the court on Friday. In the meantime, frustratingly, Layla couldn't fill in any of the gaps; all she knew was that her dad was going to the court every day and she gave the impression he was anxious about the result.

Bill seemed particularly affected by Jack's death. He didn't appear from his bedroom/study for several days and Ava had started to take his dinner down to him, so he could eat alone. She had also called Sal several times, saying soothing things and offering to help with the funeral arrangements. The house was very quiet and it felt like a black cloud was stuck directly above us all.

After what seemed like an eternity, Shawn came to pick me up on Friday with news of events so far. I jumped in his car, keen to hear the latest.

"Carlos filled me in on the days I had missed; more specialists and police witnesses attesting to Miss Avery's state of mind, and he said there were some really gory details about how the gunshot wound had killed the victim. Despite Miss Avery calling the emergency services herself, doctors said Mr Roberts would not have survived if they had got there any quicker. Then there had been a lot of technical stuff about the distance between the defendant and the victim – apparently she was really close when she shot him, again suggesting a struggle between the two. But I think the best bit and most crucial thing that happened today was when the Police Commissioner was cross-examined by the Defence. He was asked about a white box that was found in the victim's office."

I took a sharp intake of breath – they found it! "What did they say about it?"

"If you let me finish I'll tell you. So they asked the Commissioner why there hadn't been further investigation into the fact that the original box – that had already been proven to be where the bullets came from – was found in the victim's office. He seemed a bit flustered to be honest and all he could reply was that as they didn't find any DNA or fingerprints of the victim on the weapon or the box, the investigating team had thought the box had been placed there by the accused in an effort to cover her tracks."

"Surely this was enough to prove the weapon belonged to Luke Roberts though?" I asked.

"Well, the Defence said really loudly and sarcastically directly at the jury, *'so the police decide who is guilty and who is not now do they?'* and a few of the jurors and public sniggered. They then spent the rest of the day focussed solely on this box and attempting to prove how difficult it would be for Miss Avery to have planted the evidence and how it substantiated her side of events – that the gun she used had belonged to the victim and that she had found and used it in a desperate moment to save her own life."

Well, I felt relief that my contribution of planting the box had made such a significant influence on the trial. I didn't feel quite so desperate to confess my part in this whole terrible ordeal just yet – at least not until the jury had come to a decision. We drove back home poring over the details once again. It felt good to get on with Shawn for a change, putting all that previous silly, childish sibling rivalry behind us.

"Will you go back next week?" I asked him.

"Carlos thinks it will be the closing statements on Monday afternoon, then the jury will be excused to deliberate on their verdict. I would like to hear the closing statements but I'm not sure I can miss another day of school."

"Pleeeeease," I whined.

"I'll see. Carlos gave me his phone number in case I couldn't make it, so he can fill me in. I would need to call him in the evening though, without the oldies knowing so you might have to help on that front."

"Okay," I agreed.

As it happened, when Shawn picked me up from school on Monday he hadn't managed to get over to the court, so he would have to call Carlos in the evening. The landlines were situated in the 'cat room' next to the kitchen, the lounge, the main bedroom and the study. If you knew someone was on the phone in another room it was possible to pick up the receiver in a different room and listen in. Ava often did it to Bill when he was talking to Jane. I don't know why she tortured herself with knowing the depths of his devotion. Maybe it was guilt at having sent her away all those years ago – on both their parts.

When Ava had dished up the dinner, and was about to take Bill's down to him, I said, "Why don't you take yours down as well tonight and keep Bill company? Shawn and I can eat ours here together then do the washing-up for you after. I have loads of homework to do, so need to just eat quickly anyway."

Then Shawn chipped in, "I don't think it's a good idea letting Dad eat alone every night. It will lead to bad habits."

"Oh, yes okay then; thank you. You two are thoughtful," Ava said in a monotonous tone. I think she had gone beyond trying to make conversation with us every night anyway.

Once she had left the room with the two dinners, I told Shawn to make the call. He carefully lifted the receiver and dialled the number Carlos had given him.

"Hello? Carlos, it's Shawn. I'm sorry I didn't make it in to the court today. I just wondered if you could fill me in on what happened." Then a long silence as Carlos must have been speaking. I just sat motionless in front of my dinner eagerly waiting for Shawn to reply.

"Oh wow, I really wish I had seen that." Then more silence. "Yea, sure…okay, thanks, mate. Hopefully see you then."

Shawn gently put the receiver down and came and sat back at the table. "Well?!" I spat out. My heart was in my mouth as I waited for Shawn to tell me what had happened.

"Well, they made the closing statements today as expected. The Prosecution went on about the lack of proof that the gun had belonged to Luke Roberts, and that although Miss Avery had indeed suffered with his abuse, instead of going to the authorities, had acquired a weapon and planned to kill her boyfriend. Apparently they ended by saying *'don't be fooled into believing this pretty young lady is anything but a cold and calculating murderer.'* While the Defence talked about how various specialists had confirmed that an individual can be pushed beyond their limit, and in a moment of mental stress commit such an act in self-defence, they ended with this fantastic punch: *'The Prosecution has been unable to prove that the weapon did not in fact belong to the victim and therefore there is reasonable doubt to answer the case of murder.'* Then the judge summed up, instructing the jury to consider the evidence of the acquisition of the weapon, and the stress that had led to the incident. He reminded them that Miss Avery had admitted to shooting Luke Roberts, but they needed to be absolutely sure that she had planned to do so for her to be convicted of murder rather than manslaughter. He then sent the jurors off to consider their verdict."

Wow. How dare the Prosecution try to label her a murderer? "What does Carlos think?" I asked. It was difficult to predict the mood in the room with this second-hand information.

"He just said it was very dramatic and both sides were convincing. It's not a really complicated case so jurors usually reach a decision within a day. They announce over the loudspeaker when the jury are ready, and then anyone involved with the case can go to the right courtroom. I've arranged to meet Carlos there for a coffee on Wednesday morning anyway; hopefully they will make the announcement while I'm there."

"You seem to have made a new friend," I teased.

"Yes, he's nice," Shawn replied, looking down and going a bit red.

Just then we heard Ava approaching, so we quickly stuffed our dinners down.

"Oh, haven't you both finished yet?" she asked as she came into the kitchen.

"No, we've been chatting away," I answered, and Ava, still set on autopilot, ignored us and started the washing-up.

CHAPTER 15

At three on Tuesday morning I woke up in a hot sweat. I had been dreaming that I was killing people with a huge machete: one after the other, they were dying with a single swish of my weapon. Bodies were piled up like a wall, and all the time a ginger cat calmly just sat and watched me. He seemed to be in charge, but I was still wary of him. Then I found myself walking through a warehouse full of almost dead fish before I woke up confused and exhausted. I spent the rest of the night just drifting in and out of sleep before finally settling back down just before the alarm went off.

Shawn dropped me off at school in the morning; well, he did most days now as Ava didn't leave the house much anymore unless it was a food shop day, which today wasn't.

"If there is any delay in court today, don't worry about me; I'll just wait in the library until you get here. Don't miss the verdict!" I instructed Shawn before leaving his car.

"Yes, fine, Cat. Go on, or we'll both be late."

The news that the trial was likely to be decided today had spread throughout the school. Of course, Shawn had mentioned that some of the teachers had been giving evidence, so I guess they were tracking events. In the classroom there was a low hum of chatter assessing what the verdict might be. Layla seemed confident Miss Avery would receive a life sentence. "My dad said that the Defence team tried to prove that the gun belonged to her boyfriend, but even so she still knew that by using it she would kill him. It's not like she was mentally unstable or anything."

"But he was attacking her!" I replied angrily, defending Piper. "Surely that's a good enough reason!"

"Yes, maybe. If the jury decide she is not guilty of murder then it will be up to the judge to decide her fate. I hope she doesn't get a life sentence; I really did quite like her."

So, now I was worried again. Layla's dad would be very familiar with this sort of case and probably knew better than anyone what the likely outcome was. My hands were all sweaty and my stomach was feeling all twisted again. I couldn't go through the whole day thinking about this; I needed something to distract me. Since Miss Avery had been detained, our art lessons had consisted of various teachers just sitting in but today they had managed to find a proper supply teacher who could actually teach art. His name was Mr Cartwright. Pretty average looking in size and stature, adorned in typical brown trousers and jacket, a textured, corduroy looking thin tie loosely done up over a cotton shirt with the top button undone, and in need of a good ironing. He had slightly greasy hair with a few bits untidily poking up, and the look of having shaved in a rush with an electric razor as several areas of random stubble were clearly visible.

"Who thinks an art trip might be a good idea?" he asked the class. Delighted at the prospect, everyone cheered, but I knew his game. He was after Piper's job. It was too early to advertise her position yet but that was just a formality. Whatever the outcome of the trial poor Piper's teaching career was over. If Mr Cartwright got enough pupils onside before any interview process, the position would be his. Well, good luck to him, I thought. He didn't seem too bad and I had definitely had worse teachers.

"What sort of trip would you prefer? A gallery trip to look at famous paintings or a sketching trip, so you can make your own? Have a think and write down your finest idea on a piece of paper before the end of the lesson then I'll go through them and suggest the best one to Mrs Markell."

What would Piper suggest? I wondered. I decided to write down The National Gallery, so I could see some other paintings by Goya like the one sitting in a wooden box at the back of Bill's study cupboard that no one except me knew about.

Finally, Shawn turned up to collect me at five-thirty. This time I couldn't even look at him or speak; I was so worried what the verdict was.

"Manslaughter. Five years," Shawn said with a large grin on his face before he even started the car.

I was stunned. "So…so she wasn't found guilty of murder?" I finally spat out.

"Nope. The jury said she was not guilty of murder but of the lesser charge of manslaughter. The judge then said he would sentence her to five years in prison. He said she was also a victim in this terrible case and should not have her whole life tainted by the evil of Luke Roberts and the abuse she had already suffered at his hand."

"So they decided that she hadn't acquired the gun herself?"

"Not enough evidence to suggest she did, apparently. Carlos watched it all with me; we are going to meet again, so he can advise me how I could still apply to do law. I really enjoyed meeting him and seeing this case."

He started the car and began the journey home. And that was it. After what seemed like endless waiting and worrying, finally I was in the clear. The origin of the gun would never need to come out. Piper would probably be out of prison in a couple of years on probation, and be able to have a fresh start. I don't know if you can ever be free from the guilt of taking another person's life, but the main thing was that she would be free to try. Deep down I still felt guilty about the part I had played in all this. I had supplied the means for Piper to commit the crime. I should be behind bars with her. Perhaps I should write to her; I wonder if they open a prisoner's mail. Probably. I couldn't risk it, I decided. I might have to think up some way of communicating via code. I could post her a blank postcard of a forest with the words *thanks for a great day* simply written on the back. My mind was miles away when Shawn announced, "Here we are. So we are quits now remember? No more favours and no mentioning that driving incident, okay?"

"Yea, no worries, Shawn. Thanks."

When we got inside Ava told us that Jack's funeral would be the following Monday afternoon. We weren't expected to attend but Bill wanted to go and Ava might need some help to get him in the car. Bill had only been out in the car a few times since he'd been home and it was quite an ordeal. He had to slide across from his wheelchair into the car seat then someone (Ava) had to fold up his wheelchair, and put it in the car boot. Then do the whole routine backwards the other end. Ava was quite a petite person and Bill was completely the opposite, so it was a bit of a challenge. Ava complained about the weight of the wheelchair and lifting it into the boot, and Bill clearly hated relying on her and was keen to make some new arrangement as soon as he was able.

"Shawn, if you can just pop home from school at lunchtime to help that will do. Terry can help with the wheelchair at the church."

"You want me to drive all the way back here just to put the wheelchair in the boot? That will be like a forty-minute round trip plus the actual job. There won't be any point in me going back to school, but as long as you have a few seconds help!" Shawn shouted.

"If it's too much to ask then don't worry yourself!" Ava retorted almost in tears. I hadn't noticed her being so emotional previously. Most of the time she just appeared detached and in her own world. I felt angry; it's not like it was her that couldn't walk. Even Shawn who had always been her precious favourite looked annoyed.

There was a moment's silence while Ava looked truly hurt before Shawn caved in, "Fine. I'll be back by one-fifteen."

The news of the trial spread through school without the need for me to fill anyone in. The evening of the verdict it had featured on the local news: a brief glimpse of Piper arriving in court and an old photo of her when she graduated were all they could find to represent her. They filled in the gaps with pictures of her home, and of course an interview with Luke's family stating they were very disappointed with the verdict and would never forgive Piper for the pain she had caused them. Piper's solicitor made a statement saying he was pleased the jury had made the right decision in a case where there were in fact two victims. Piper must have been taken to her new cell; all eyes on the new girl as she walked nervously through the prison. I hoped she would toughen up quickly. I could imagine her being bullied in there just as she had been by Luke but now lacking the weapon to aid her.

So the art teacher position was officially available, and the school would be keen to fill it without attracting too much further attention. Our class teacher casually asked us during registration what we thought of Mr Cartwright and most students nodded and said he was okay. His plan to quickly fill the position would be successful – and as long as he fulfilled his bribe to take us on a trip, I guess we would all be happy. And if I really wanted to go to art school I would need a proper educator to guide me rather than endless supply teachers.

True to his word, during the next art lesson Mr Cartwright announced the trip would be to The National Gallery. There were a few groans around the classroom, and Katie shouted from the back, "How boring. Who suggested that?"

"All suggestions were anonymous, Katie, and it was Mrs Markell who decided. Anyway, it will be great, going up to London and seeing paintings by the great masters will be inspirational!" declared Mr Cartwright. I kept quiet that it was my idea. I'd rather be sharing the trip with Piper, but I was looking forward to seeing some more work by Goya.

Jack's funeral came and went without much mention. I assumed Shawn fulfilled his duty; I forgot to ask him.

A few weeks later a new car appeared on the drive, delivered by one of the mechanics from the garage. I watched from the window upstairs as Bill wheeled himself around the vehicle. The mechanic – I think his name was Paulo – opened the driver's door wide and Bill wheeled himself up to the seat. Paulo went to help him but Bill waved him away. I couldn't hear what he said but from his body language it looked like he wanted to tackle this alone. He pulled out a polished plank of wood from the back of his wheelchair, and wedged it under his thigh resting the other end on the car seat. Next he reached inside the roof of the car door for the handle and grabbed it with his right hand. He then began the slow process of shifting a leg into the car with his left hand. Then he tried to slide himself across the plank and into the seat. Finally, he lifted his remaining leg into the car before adjusting himself, so he was comfortable in the driving seat. It was painful to watch, his slow movements making a mockery of the man he used to be. Once in the car Paulo folded up the wheelchair and put it in the boot. After that he got into the passenger seat and Bill started the car and slowly they left the drive. I wondered how he was working the pedals but I would have to wait until a closer inspection of the car to find out.

As I ventured downstairs I heard Ava on the phone. "Yes I know you can only discuss this with Bill, but I don't think he's telling me the truth. He believes he is going to walk again and I just want to know the realistic chances of that happening. I have a right to know. It's me that's doing all the care and I need to know how long it will be for."

Her voice was shaking, sounding desperate even. It was the question we all wanted the answer to. There was a long silence while she listened. "I see…yes I understand; to be honest I did think that was the case. Do you think he should see a counsellor? To help him come to terms with the prognosis? He tells everyone and anyone that will listen that he will soon be back on his feet again. It's like he's in complete denial."

Then there was another long pause but I didn't bother to eavesdrop any more. I could deduce from this snippet of conversation that Bill would never walk again despite his insistence that he would. And Ava was right: we did all know this deep down. It was only Bill's positive attitude that had us questioning the facts. Maybe it was better to let him hold onto that thought; perhaps it was his way of dealing with it. Either way, this life we all now led was set to remain the same for the foreseeable future.

A few hours later I heard a car horn beeping outside. I looked out the porch window and saw Bill had pulled up outside. I waved and went out. He was alone in the car; Paulo must have been dropped off.

"What do you think of this?" he asked me.

"Yea, it's cool. How does it work?"

"Paulo fitted a handle to the steering wheel here that operates the pedals, so I can work the car with my hands. It's actually very simple; he's a clever chap. What I want to do now is reverse the vehicle into the carport so that I can line myself up with a wheelchair. Then I can keep a wheelchair permanently in the car, and leave the house here without needing anyone's help. When I get to work, one of the guys can take it out the boot for me. So are you strong enough to take one of the wheelchairs out the boot?"

I went around to the rear of the car and popped the boot open. There were two wheelchairs piled on top of each other. I tried to lift one out. I wasn't prepared for how heavy it was, and to make it worse it had somehow become joined to the one below.

"Come on – use some muscle!" Bill called from within. He was clearly delighted with his new adapted mobility and I didn't want to let him down.

With a big effort I managed to wedge half the chair on the edge of the boot, then I lifted the wheels up and out onto the ground, the top crashing down after them. I could see why Ava complained so much; it was a very difficult job. It was out though, and I opened it up and manoeuvred it over to Bill.

"Ah what I want you to do is wheel it round to the carport. I'm going to reverse the car up to it, so place it roughly where you think the car door opening will be."

I did as instructed. Luckily it was a double carport so there was plenty of room. Bill began to reverse the car towards me. As he got nearer, he opened his car door wide and slowly manoeuvred the car alongside the wheelchair. Initially he wasn't quite close enough, so he moved in and out a couple of times before he was as close to the wheelchair as possible. Then he used his plank of wood to slide himself into the chair.

"There, how about that?" he said triumphantly. "Now I can go out whenever I want."

It was quite clever I had to admit, and good to see his confidence and strength coming back. "Now you can give me a lift to school," I joked.

We went inside the house; I could tell he was keen to surprise Ava with his news. Just as we reached the hall we heard another car on the drive. "Who is that?" Bill asked me. He couldn't see out the window from his seat.

I peered outside. A silver Jaguar was parking, not a car I recognised, but as a tall man got out and strode confidently towards the front door, I knew exactly who it was. "Jack's son, Charles."

Bill went to open the door before Charles needed to knock. "Hello, young man," he greeted Charles in an upbeat way, still feeling cheerful after his car success.

"Afternoon, Bill," Charles replied in his cold, formal manner. "Can we talk?"

"Of course. Come through to the lounge. Fancy a drink?"

"No thank you."

Charles was so cold and calculating, the complete opposite of his father Jack; not that I had liked him much either, just for different reasons. Bill wheeled himself into the lounge and Charles followed after giving me a thin smile and a piercing look as if to suggest I was not welcome to follow. I turned and noisily made my way upstairs, so he would think I was out of the way. Once he was out of sight, I crept back down so their conversation was within earshot.

Charles was talking. "Now I've fully taken over Dad's business, I've noticed some discrepancies in your accounts. According to the records, it seems you owe the firm a substantial amount of money. Now, of course, I understand this has been a difficult time for you, Bill, and you and Jack were good friends, but I cannot allow this kind of behaviour to continue."

Bill interrupted. "What are you talking about? Jack had been keeping all my surplus earnings; I've given him over four hundred thousand in cash! He said you had invested it in a fictitious property in order to hide it away from the tax man. ABC Cars it was called. As it happens, I needed the money back to pay for things while I've been laid up and I was going to talk to him about it…the day he came over, but…well, you know what happened that day."

"There is nothing to do with a company in that name. I've never heard of it," Charles said in his serious, monotone voice. He carried on, "All I can see from the books is that you haven't paid the last two invoices. I assumed Dad was not chasing because of your…situation, but now I am in charge, could I ask you to call the office and finalise your debt?"

"Look, young man, it's out of my respect for your father that I don't raise my voice with you. I'm telling you that it's YOU that owes ME money, MY money! I need it now to pay for all this. Go back to your office and have a proper look."

"Calm down, Bill. So, just for argument's sake, exactly how did you give Jack all this money?" Charles continued, unrattled by Bill's anger.

Bill sounded noticeably distressed. "In cash payments, over the last few years. Look, Jack sorted it all so it was kosher. He said it was complicated and he would deal with it to help me avoid tax. His cut was eight per cent. Then all this happened, and I just haven't thought about it until now. I really need that money back, Charles. Richard has been running things at the garage and according to him trade has taken a bit of a downturn. Now I have my car though, I'll soon be back to work to get things moving. It's just that this has all cost me quite a lot. The nurses and physio, the specialist equipment and everything; I'm running very short."

"I understand your situation, Bill, and how quick it can be to fall into debt. I know Dad was very fond of you but he wouldn't have just taken four hundred thousand pounds of your money, and risked imprisonment just to avoid some tax. When I am back in the office I'll check for anything relating to this company, ABC Cars. In the meantime, if you could give Tanya a ring in the office and settle your account that would be great."

As Charles made his speech, his voice was getting louder. He was moving towards making an exit. I ascended the stairs quietly before I was seen. I just made it onto the landing before I heard the front door open and close. He must have let himself out, not wanting to discuss the matter further. I didn't believe for a moment Charles wasn't aware of the company ABC Cars; he was clearly lying to Bill, but why?

I went back down and peeped through the door to the lounge. Bill was still there, his back to me, head down in his hands. I couldn't see his face but his shoulders were shaking up and down. Suddenly he made a loud snorting noise and I realised he was crying. I had never seen him cry; he was always so strong. It was such a strange sight. My instinct was to go and console him, but I held back. He would be embarrassed and ashamed if he knew I was watching. I was so captivated with the scene I didn't hear Ava come up behind me. "Who are you spying on?"

I whipped round. "Oh, you made me jump." I turned to look at her then immediately back to look at Bill, aware I had probably been rumbled. The sound of voices made Bill quickly wipe his face and wheel himself around to face us. Pulling a great big smile, he said, "Oh, you just missed Charles. He told me the funniest joke; made me cry with laughter."

I looked down at my feet. I didn't want to make him feel uncomfortable by staring at his teary face. "I'm going up to my room to finish my homework."

"Don't you want to hear the joke?" Ava asked. But before I could answer Bill said, "It's a bit rude." Well, that put an end to that, and she let me go.

CHAPTER 16

Over the next six months Bill started going back to work daily. His new routine kicked off with an early breakfast, then while Ava was getting him ready I would sort my own breakfast out, usually alone. My sixteenth birthday came and went without much celebration; I didn't want any fuss – my mind wishing the years away until I would be old enough to move out anyway.

I didn't hear about any more visits from Charles, and noticing Bill's mood I assumed he still wasn't going to receive the money he was owed. I did recall Jack's conversation about ABC Cars with Bill but of course no one knew I was privy to it, and I wouldn't be believed anyway. A melancholy filled the air of the home. It was as if a permanent rain cloud was above all our heads and there was no break to allow a ray of sunshine through.

Ava continued on autopilot. Billie-Joe was hardly ever around at home, and certainly wouldn't be visiting the business any time soon now he knew Richard would always be there. I don't know what he did or where he went. He just seemed to turn up irregularly, often with a new girlfriend in tow, stinking of cheap aftershave, and with eyes that looked like a zombie's. Shawn had started going out a lot more. Ava teased him about whether he had found a girlfriend at last. I knew he was seeing Carlos but said nothing; how could his own mother be so blind? One evening Bill came in from work looking particularly annoyed. Shawn was out and without even acknowledging me he launched into a rant at Ava.

"Richard has fired my secretary Carol! Can you believe it? Carol has worked for me loyally for fifteen years, and he has just unilaterally decided she has to go. I know he has been running things for me and times have been hard of late but to just fire someone like that; it's just not the way to operate."

"Did he say why he fired her?" Ava asked.

"Yes of course. He explained we have to make cutbacks, and it seems poor Carol is one of them. When I spoke to her she told me not to worry as she would have more time to spend with the grandkids now, and it was about time she retired anyway. April has offered to come in on Saturday mornings while her mum has the baby and go through all the accounting for the week in a couple of hours, which is very kind of her, I suppose. Richard has updated the computer system so things can work more efficiently, but of course I just don't understand it now. Computers are a young person's tool and without Carol to explain things for me I'll never be able to work it out."

"It sounds to me like Carol didn't really mind being fired. I'm sure Richard is simply looking out for you, and it's no bad thing for you to take a step back and let someone else take the strain for a bit, so you can concentrate on yourself."

"I just feel like a spare part in my own business. Richard keeps telling me how bad trade is, and it seems there is nothing I can do to help. I can't even demonstrate the vehicles to customers any more from this stupid position. He's also let Beryl the cleaner go, so the place will soon be looking dirty."

I interjected here. "I can come and clean on Saturdays. I've been thinking about getting a Saturday job anyway. My rate will be half what Beryl's was!" I added with a smile.

Bill turned to look at me as if he'd only just realised I was in the room. "Er sure; thanks, Cat, that would be a help."

I got up and left the room before Ava could object with some sarcastic comment like '*I didn't think you knew how to clean.*'

It seemed like the money problems were worse than I'd realised.

When Saturday came around I got up as if it was a school day. Normally I would turn my alarm off so I could have a lie-in, but today I was going to be cleaning. I hadn't been back up to the car showroom since the incident but today I felt determined to put that behind me and help out. Bill drove me up to the showroom in silence. I could tell his mind was miles away, thinking about what had happened during the week. When we arrived I retrieved his wheelchair for him and he slid into it. He was much quicker at it now he'd had so much practice. He wheeled away into the showroom and I followed. Richard had already opened up and was busy with an early bird couple. I went to the small kitchen area to get the cleaning stuff.

All the things I needed were there under the sink. I put the Marigolds on first, and started the pile of washing-up that was there. I hadn't done much when April appeared behind me.

"Bill said you were coming in to 'help'." She said the words so coldly and with such hatred it was as if it was hard for her to spit them out at all.

"Oh well yes, I'm going to help with some cleaning on Saturdays – a bit like you with the accounts," I replied smiling, hoping I could break through whatever was bothering her about me being there.

Just then Richard emerged behind April and put his arm around her shoulders. Holding her tightly he jovially asked, "Everything okay, you two?"

April shrugged him off and went back to her desk without a word, just leaving me with a final menacing look. What was her problem? I thought. I looked blankly at Richard, and gave him a weak smile. "April is just a bit tired with the new baby; just ignore her, and perhaps give her a wide berth for now," he said before turning to follow April into the office where he leant over and seemed to whisper something in her ear before returning to his customers.

Richard wasn't particularly friendly either, and as I began scrubbing the coffee cups I tried to remember the last time I had seen them. It was before April had given birth – that's right, she was still pregnant and they had both come over to see Bill and Ava and talk babies. That was when Billie-Joe burst in and then abruptly left again when he saw Richard was there. Then I remembered the split second when Richard's face went white after shaking hands with Billie-Joe. He must have twigged in that exact moment. Maybe he recognised him or something about him in that brief encounter that jogged his brain into recalling that terrible day he was held up at gunpoint and tied to a tree, losing his dignity and livelihood all in one go. Oh God; if they knew it was Billie-Joe who planned the holdup then they must know it was me who divulged the information from Richard's diary the night of their party. How else could Billie-Joe have known the exact time and place Richard would be there with the Bugatti? But if they really had worked all that out, then why hadn't they gone to the police? Or at least confronted Bill. Why were they both happily working here and doing their best to help him out? As I spent the morning cleaning whilst trying desperately to avoid them both, the conundrum just went round and round in my head. Why, why, why?

At noon Bill called me to go home. The garage was only open Saturday mornings and Richard had already started locking up. I slipped out the back and waited by the car while Bill said his thanks and goodbyes to April before following me around to the car. I put his wheelchair in the boot without a word and we started the journey home. After ten minutes I asked, "Do you think Richard likes working for you?"

"That's a strange question," Bill replied. "I don't know if he likes selling cars, but we've been friends for years, and I guess after all…that business, he's pleased for the job."

I was quiet for a few more minutes before plucking up the courage to ask about that business. I didn't want to bring it up, and knew I was never meant to speak about it, but it was just me and Bill in the car so… "Do you think Richard will ever find out what really happened? You know…with the holdup and Billie-Joe and everything."

"What makes you ask that?" Bill replied abruptly. "How could he ever find out? Anyway, that's all history; he's got the baby to concentrate on now, and he's practically running the business single-handed since I gave him a job when no one else would."

"Yes but you only gave him the job because you felt guilty." As soon as the words had left my mouth I realised I pushed it a bit too far.

"That's enough! I told you not to mention that. It's all in the past now, I don't want you to talk about this again – do you understand?"

His words were final. I knew the tone: I would have to drop it. It didn't mean I wouldn't still be wondering about it though. I needed to get to the reason why Richard hadn't been to the police – yet.

Finally, it was time for the school trip to The National Gallery. I was probably the only person looking forward to it but any kind of school trip was a good one really. The coach was buzzing all the way to London as we shared sweets and stories. Mr Cartwright was being accompanied by the music teacher, Mrs Beauchamp. They sat at the front, deep in conversation, and pretty much ignoring the riot that was going on behind them in the coach. As we pulled up at the gallery he gave out instructions about meeting up in the foyer at three, and apart from that we were to stay inside the gallery at all times. We were free to roam anywhere inside but must make a pencil study of a painting of our choosing. Everyone linked arms with a friend and launched off into the building giggling and almost running. Layla hadn't come on the trip, so I was left alone. It didn't matter though; I knew where I wanted to go. I collected a map and asked at the reception where I could find paintings by Goya. An overkeen girl wearing a nametag saying INTERN Julia, circled the room *Paintings After 1600* on my map, and sent me off in the right direction.

I quickly found the room and scanned along the wall of paintings before I came to one by Francisco de Goya. I walked on past to see how many paintings there were by Goya altogether. There were only four: three formal looking portraits which didn't look like they were even by the same artist, and one small painting called 'A Picnic'. This one was more along the lines of the one I had seen all that time ago: the one that was still buried deep inside our cupboard at home. Since the study had become Bill's bedroom and the huge old oak desk had been wedged in front of the sliding cupboard doors, I knew the painting couldn't have been moved.

The character in the centre of 'A Picnic' had the same cheeky looking face as the man refuelling the oil lamp that I had seen before. This was the painting that I decided to make my sketch of. The room was fairly void of people, just the odd tourist or pensioner passing by. There was a bench in the middle of the room, so I settled down there and got out my sketchbook and pencil. The seat was a bit further away than I would have liked, so I had to keep getting up to have a closer look at the details.

The scene featured seven figures, all seated on the ground with the remains of a picnic. On the right of the foreground a man lay on the ground, his head in his hands, looking rather the worse for wear. Opposite him was a beautiful lady – the sick man's fiancée I imagined – but right in the middle of the painting and obviously trying to woo her was one of Goya's gargoyle-looking characters. He had more personality than the other figures, and sat full of confidence with his arms and legs spread wide. I could tell she didn't like his advances as she coyly looked away. Behind him, and in the background, the other figures giggled amongst themselves at his efforts. Although painted in 1798, a similar scene could have happened today.

I spent all day in the same spot. At two-thirty I sat back down on the bench to pack away my things. Just before I rose to leave, a tour group came in the room. They stopped in front of the Goya paintings blocking my view.

"Now, how many of you are familiar with the work of Francisco de Goya?" the tour guide asked them.

There were a few mumbles from the group.

"Perhaps some of you remember hearing on the news about the robbery of 'The Forcibly Bewitched' by Goya whilst being transported here to the gallery?"

Now the group perked up with louder mutters and nods. My interest also doubled and my head shot up to look at the guide and I gave her my full attention.

"Did anyone hear on the news that the stolen painting has in fact been recovered?"

I was absolutely speechless. How had they recovered it? As far as I knew it was still sitting in Bill's bedroom and it was the same question on the group's lips. "Where did they find it?" they asked almost in unison.

"The painting was actually found purely by accident when the police carried out a major drugs raid at the billionaire Jacob Charters' home in Chelsea. They discovered a whole load of stolen goods at the same time! Numerous artefacts have been recovered including 'The Forcibly Bewitched'. For anyone desperate to see it today, it is currently on temporary display in The Central Hall until this room is re-hung and it can be put in its rightful place alongside Goya's other works."

The painting had been here all day! I had to see it with my own eyes. Was the forgery really so good that even the gallery experts didn't spot it? I retrieved my map to locate The Central Hall and set off at a fast pace. I had to go up to Level 2, and I didn't have much time left before three o'clock and the end of the trip. When I located the right room, 'The Forcibly Bewitched' was hanging right by the stairs. There was a temporary notice on the wall next to it that simply read:

Francisco de Goya

A Scene from El Hechizado por Fuerza ('The Forcibly Bewitched')

1798

And that was all. No explanation about where the painting had been or how it was stolen in the first place. I wondered if under police questioning the billionaire had given up Ed's name although I knew Ed would never mention Bill, and anyway as far as he was aware he had sold the original and not the fake. He didn't know I had swapped them – no one did. Suddenly I felt a burst of laughter. It came out as a loud coughing sound as I tried to hold it back. The security guard gave me a warning look, so I quickly composed myself. Here in front of me on display for all the world to see was not a two-hundred-year-old work by one of the greatest and most influential of the Old Masters ever, but a fake by Ed's friend Nicholas.

All the way back on the coach I had a smile on my face. I had always been a bit of a rebel and loved beating the powers that be, but this time – wow, what an achievement!

CHAPTER 17

The months rolled on. I cleaned on Saturdays, being very careful to avoid Richard and April. Bill gave me £10 each week as payment, a token gesture really considering the work I got done in those three hours, but I didn't complain. I started saving it towards driving lessons. Since Shawn had been able to drive I had been very jealous of his ability to come and go as he pleased, and now I yearned for that freedom too. He had his own Saturday job now as well and would be going to university soon, so I wouldn't be able to use him for lifts any more either.

For as long as I can remember, behind the mechanics' area at the business, there was a deep burgundy coloured Morris Minor parked. One Saturday, as we arrived for work, I asked Bill whose it was.

"It's mine. I won it off someone in a bet years ago but I never got around to fixing it up," he said.

"After I learn to drive can I use it?"

"What would you want that old thing for? Wouldn't you prefer a fast little run-around like Shawn?"

"No. I really want that one," I pleaded, tilting my head and making my eyes go in that 'Daddy's girl' way.

"Well yes, I guess so. I'll ask Paulo to fix it up when he has any spare time."

Now I was excited. I imagined driving off into the sunset in my burgundy Morris Minor, sunglasses on and all the boys looking my way.

When we got inside the showroom, a rather worried looking Richard came straight up to Bill.

"April isn't in today. Rosie has been up all night and has a rash this morning. April didn't want to leave her." He looked tired.

Bill said, "I'm sure she'll be fine. Kids bounce back incredibly fast after they have been ill."

Richard just nodded and shuffled off to his office.

A couple of hours later, after I'd cleaned the toilets and kitchen, I was dusting in the showroom when Bill said to Richard, "It's been a quiet morning and you won't be able to focus on the customers anyway in this state; just go home and check on the family. I can manage for the last couple of hours."

"Are you sure?" Richard asked, but he was already putting his jacket on, desperate to go.

"Yes, Cat can help me close up. Give me a ring tomorrow to let me know how she is."

Richard practically ran out to his car and drove off without another word.

A few minutes later a customer came in. Bill did his best to show them around the cars then took them to his office to discuss things further. I finished my jobs early and put the cleaning things away by which time the customers were leaving. Bill wheeled himself out the office looking downhearted.

"What happened?" I asked.

"They wanted me to check stock levels for the metallic blue but I couldn't understand how to even switch the computer on, so just had to write down their details so Richard can get back to them next week. When I was running the place I used to keep a paper copy in the file."

"I've finished the cleaning so why don't I give you a basic computer lesson? At least I'll teach you how to switch it on!"

Bill thought about my offer for a moment before asking, "Do you know how to use it? I don't want to mess up any of Richard's files."

"Of course. Don't worry; I use them all the time at school."

We went to Richard's office. The computer was set up at his desk and I sat down in his chair, moving it across so Bill could wheel in next to me. "So, the first thing you need to do is switch it on here," I said, feeling around the back for the on button. The screen lit up asking for a password. "Ah, he has a password on it. Do you know it?" I asked.

"No. I have no idea. I could give him a ring…but I'd rather not bother him. Never mind, I'll ask him next week."

"Well we could have a few guesses first," I said. I was keen to have a look on his computer now, and I really wanted to help Bill out. I typed in RICHARD but the password box just rejected that. Next I tried APRIL – nope, ROSIE – nope, BABYROSIE – nope. Hmm, what would he use? I carried on with various combinations including birthdays and ages and years. None of them let me in.

"We'll have to leave it," Bill said. "Come on, let's go home early. I'm not going to be much use here today." He wheeled himself away and towards the mechanics' area; he looked very low. There wouldn't be anyone out there today and I think he just needed a few moments on his own. I had noticed his eyes watering several times recently before he took himself off out of sight. I think he was crying again.

I turned my attention back to the computer screen. One last thought occurred to me. I slowly typed in the letters B U G A T T I and like magic the screen changed to a photo of April and Rosie; I was in.

I debated calling Bill back but decided to let him have a bit of time alone. Little icons were stacked across the screen. I opened the documents and a long list of folders presented itself. I scanned down the page, astonished at all the names and information that was on the screen. I looked down the list slowly at all the titles, 'advertising', 'invoices', 'stock', 'staff'. The list went on. Then I came to one titled 'private', and that was the one I chose to open.

A new page was now on the display with a folder titled 'Bugatti'. I hovered the cursor over the name; the file was an Excel Worksheet. I hesitated opening it, wondering about its contents. The uncertainty soon passed and I clicked on it. The time it took for the spreadsheet to load seemed endless. I already had my suspicions that Richard and April knew about the theft, but to actually have a file on it seemed very peculiar and now I desperately needed to know what was inside.

Once open, I studied the contents. Across the top of the columns the headings read: DATE, MODEL, LIST PRICE, NET CUSTOMER PRICE, VAT, RICHARD CASH. Then, the boxes underneath were full of figures starting from about six months ago. I picked up a calculator from the desk; the RICHARD CASH figure was always the difference between NET CUSTOMER PRICE and LIST PRICE.

My forehead was rippled with concentration. What did it mean? I minimised the spreadsheet and went back to the long list of folders. I scanned down them again before finding one titled 'Income and Expenses'. I clicked it open to reveal more spreadsheets, each dated with a month. I selected MARCH. Once it was loaded I looked for the sales income. Along the tabs at the bottom was one labelled SALES. Up came the March car sales worksheet, again with headings along the top. This time they read: DATE, MODEL, TOTAL PAID, PURCHASE PRICE, COMMISSION, VAT, NET. Then the boxes underneath were filled out with about fifteen rows of sales. After studying this page for several minutes I brought up the first spreadsheet and put the two side by side on the monitor, so I could compare the figures. I didn't quite understand what all these figures meant yet, but what I could deduce was that Richard seemed to be creaming off about £30,000 per month as at the bottom of the Bugatti worksheet the figures were all added up, and RICHARD CASH column said £178,963.

It seems he was using the maximum traders' discount for the books and taking the shortfall from the customer in cash, thus saving them the VAT. He doesn't do it with every sale, probably just the shady customers he can persuade. That certainly explains why the profits have been so bad – he's been pocketing them! This discovery also enlightened me on why he hadn't gone to the police with his suspicions about my family's involvement in the Bugatti theft. Not only was he making himself a tidy bit of money, he was also ruining the company. This was revenge. I looked at some spreadsheets from the more recent months just to make doubly sure. Not only did they clarify my suspicion, but it looked like the business was going under. Each month the debts looked worse as the figures changed into negatives.

This was probably the worst kind of punishment someone could inflict on Bill. Money was like a god to him and the company he had built up over his adult lifetime was being ruined. How could Richard be so cruel – and after he knew Bill needed money for treatment.

Just then, I heard Bill calling me to get ready to leave. I quickly looked around the office for some blank floppy disks. I spotted a pack on the shelf and took a new one out and popped it in the computer. I copied Richard's PRIVATE file, and the spreadsheets, and loaded them onto the blank disk, just to give me a bit of time to decide what to do. I couldn't exactly go to the police with this but nor could Richard either. I closed down the computer and left everything exactly as I had found it, ejecting the floppy disk and putting it in my bag.

"Come on; let's close up and go home. I just want to get out of here," Bill called again.

We closed up nearly two hours early and drove home. As we pulled into the drive, there was a silver Jaguar parked near the front. Bill recognised whose it was and muttered, "What's Charles doing here? He knows I'll be at work."

He parked the car in the carport as usual; he didn't need me to help him this end, so I went in the house. It was quiet, of course; it would only be Ava at home this time on a Saturday anyway, but where was she? And where was Charles? I went through all the downstairs rooms without any luck. As I went back into the hall, Bill wheeled in.

"I can't find them anywhere," I told him.

"Run upstairs and see if Ava is in bed with a migraine. I expect Charles went for a walk when he realised I wouldn't be back for a while."

I went upstairs, all the way along the corridor to Ava's suite. I wasn't allowed in her rooms, so it felt strange. I crept in not wanting to wake her if she was sleeping. As I approached her door I heard some muffled voices, so I stopped and peeped through the slit in the hinged side of the door. There on the bed, facing each other, half naked were Ava and Charles. I couldn't quite believe what I was seeing. My mother and that slime bag in bed together!

Ava quietly said, "We'd better get dressed, darling. Bill will only be another hour or so, and he mustn't see you here. We don't want him suspecting you have any involvement in my departure." She leaned in to kiss him. Then Charles sat up.

"Not long now, my love; as soon as you are ready we'll be able to start our new life together." They kissed again before Charles stood up and began putting his clothes on.

I felt sick and withdrew from my position undetected, and back out to the landing. They were not just having an affair, but planning to take off into the sunset together! My heart was pounding with rage. What was she thinking? Charles was horrible, despite also being years younger than her. Bill was waiting at the bottom of the stairs for me to report back, clearly unsuspecting of such a scenario; he innocently thought Charles might be 'having a walk'! What should I do? Everyone around Bill was turning on him. I couldn't let him find out about this latest betrayal in his current state of mind – if he found out right now that his wife was planning to run off with the man who had also probably stolen his money, that would just about finish him off.

I heard footsteps – Charles was coming. As soon as he stepped out of the suite, he saw me. He took a sharp breath in and was about to speak when I immediately put my finger up to my lips to signify to him not to say a word. We stood there facing each other in stunned silence. I pointed to the stairs, and did a mime of someone in a wheelchair, attempting to signal that Bill was right there below us. Next I grabbed his arm and took him further up the corridor to my room. I was fuming now. This horrible man was moments away from destroying our family life completely. But to my surprise, once inside my room Charles whispered, "Thank you, but I was just helping Ava to move a chest of drawers."

Did this man just talk in lies, I thought. To come up with one so quickly, it must be just like second nature to him.

"I'm sorry to disappoint you, Charles, but I had the unfortunate sight just now of your bare arse, and that tells me that it wasn't a chest of drawers you were moving!"

The next moment he was begging, "Please don't say anything. I have two young children and a loving wife. This fling with Ava was just a bit of fun. No one needs to get hurt, do they? I'm sorry you witnessed it but can you just try to forget all about it?"

I was gobsmacked at the man's ability to dump Ava so fast. Was he even serious about running off with her? How had she fallen for this idiot? And how on earth had he won her over with his smarmy character? I didn't know anything about his family but at that moment I felt sorry for his poor wife.

"Bill is, by the way, waiting at the bottom of the stairs for me. You won't get past him with any stupid tale about a chest of drawers either. There is only one way out of this without harming anyone: you can climb out of my window here and onto the flat roof where you can get back down to the drive. Bill has seen your car and thinks you have gone for a walk whilst waiting for him to get back from work."

Charles just looked at me blankly for a moment before he looked out the window to observe his potential escape route. "I suppose I could do that just to save anyone getting hurt," he said casually.

I thought for a moment, then replied simply, "There is one small thing I want in return from you: when you come back from your walk, you are going to tell Bill the reason you came over to see him today. You found his missing money from ABC Cars."

"What? Are you mad?!" he laughed.

"That's the deal, Charles. I would hurry up and decide if I were you; it would be such a shame for you to become one of those dads who see their children every other weekend. I've seen what damage divorce can do to kids. Believe me, paying this money back will be worth it in the long run. Once you have given Bill his money back I promise to completely forget all about seeing you naked in my mother's bed."

Charles was silent for a moment before he opened the window and peered out. "Fine," was all he could manage to say before he climbed out onto the flat roof. I had been right to suspect him; he was aware of ABC Cars.

"See you downstairs at the front door with the good news," I whispered after him.

I watched as Charles disappeared off the edge of the roof.

Now I had to deal with Ava. As I got back to her suite, Bill called up from below, "Well? What's going on up there?"

Ava stepped out at the same time and we stood face to face – hers filled with confusion and fear, and mine anger and disgust. "I'm coming down now," I called back expressionlessly. "You were right: Mum did have a bit of a headache and is lying down. She hasn't seen Charles though. As you suggested, he must be out walking whilst waiting for you to get back from work."

With that I turned my back on Ava and walked back downstairs to where Bill was waiting. Secure in the knowledge that all was well, he wheeled away down to his bedroom muttering, "Let me know when Charles arrives."

I made myself a cup of tea in the kitchen, anxious for Charles to reappear at the front door and report the good news to Bill. At least this money would keep us going while I worked out what to do about Richard. I managed to eat almost an entire packet of biscuits before the doorbell finally rang. I went straight out to the hall. Bill was already there and just then Ava began her descent from the stairs as well. I opened the door and Charles came in. Ava went as white as a sheet.

"Good morning, Bill. Apologies. I had completely forgotten you went to work on Saturday mornings, but to save me coming back I thought I would take a walk in your beautiful garden while I waited for you to return, so I could give you some news."

Here it comes, I thought.

"I have been surveying your latest accounts with our dear friend Richard, and can see you have fallen on difficult times. I really feel terrible about adding my company debt onto your worries, so I wanted to tell you to just forget all about it. You were such a good friend to Dad when he was alive, and I know he would want me to help you in any way I could.

"I just wanted to tell you personally, so that there are no hard feelings. I've had a very busy year – what with taking over the company and finalising all Dad's affairs, but now I understand how difficult this last year must have also been for you, and hope that even in the smallest of ways this will perhaps relieve your burden."

What? That's not what he was meant to say! What was he doing?

"Yes well, that is very big of you, Charles, I'm sure, although I must say that I didn't feel in any kind of debt to you anyway. Your father and I had our own arrangements as I have previously explained to you which leads me on to ask you again if you have located my money from ABC Cars." Bill scowled.

"Sadly not, Bill." Charles turned to look at me and put his hand on my shoulder, and with an awful smirk on his face added, "Try to just be grateful for the beautiful, caring family around you. Something I am yet to achieve and no amount of money can buy."

Then he turned and left without even a cursory glance at Ava.

Slowly it dawned on me that Charles had played me. There was no doting wife or small children waiting for him at home and I couldn't speak now of what I had seen a little over an hour ago – all I had managed to achieve was help him escape and secure that Ava's adultery remained secret. He wasn't going to get away with this. Now it was my turn to play dirty.

CHAPTER 18

As soon as I turned seventeen, I booked five driving lessons. Of course, I had grown up around cars and could already drive, but to be able to pass the test I would need to get rid of a few bad habits. I arranged for two lessons a week with an AA instructor called Kenny Loach. I picked him deliberately. Mia, a girl in my class, had used him and warned everyone to stay well clear. She had described how sleazy he was, leching all over her and being suggestive. She only had one lesson with him before ditching him. However, I decided to try to use this creep to my advantage. I had been thinking long and hard how to deal with Richard and Charles and now it seemed quite possible they were in cahoots anyway, perhaps there was a way I could deal with them both at the same time.

When Kenny pulled up in the drive for my lesson and I saw him for the first time, he was exactly as Mia had described: in his early thirties, slightly on the short side and with a beer belly beginning to develop. His hair was slicked back with just a bit too much wax in it, causing it to look unclean, and he was trying to achieve that designer stubble look that only the really well-groomed superstars can pull off. He pulled down his Ray-Bans to the end of his nose and said in a slow, nonchalant way, "Hey, slip into the driver's seat, so I can get you a licence."

I had opted for a fairly skimpy outfit and with a slight smile in his direction did as I was instructed. Once in the car, Kenny got into the passenger seat. My skirt was raised even further up now I was sitting down and my long bare legs were revealed.

"So, how much do I need to teach you?" he asked me – with another meaning altogether in his head, I could tell already.

I adjusted the seat and put on my seat belt. Kenny put his belt on as well.

"Quite right; safety first." Another innuendo.

I started the engine and manoeuvred the car out the driveway, stopping only briefly to check the road was clear then accelerated at speed down South Drive, rapidly changing the gears until we hit sixty miles per hour before pulling off the road and stopping at the edge of some woods in a lay-by, a dust cloud surrounding the car.

"Ah okay," Kenny laughed nervously. "I see you know quite a bit already, but you won't pass the test that way, I'm afraid."

I lowered the window and reached into my bag for some cigarettes. I lit two then passed him one. "I know. I want you to teach me how to pass. I've booked you for five lessons but if you can do it in four, then perhaps on the last one we could do something else." I gave him the most alluring and suggestive look I could.

Kenny looked slightly uneasy for a second; clearly he was used to being in charge. He took a long drag on his cigarette. "Okay, let's get you started."

Part one of my plan had begun. Kenny was hooked. He spent the next three lessons focussed almost entirely on giving me the best instructions he possibly could – with the odd hand on my knee slipped in of course. I made him book my test date for the week after my last lesson so there was no misunderstanding that I would continue with any more lessons after the final one. By the time we had completed three lessons I was rid of all my bad habits and confident that I would easily pass. I had to admit, Kenny had actually taught me quite well, and I felt a slight pang of guilt knowing how I was going to trap him.

When our fourth lesson came round Kenny ran it like a practice test, pretending to be all official with a clipboard and the whole shebang right from the start. As soon as we finished and I stopped the engine, he came out of character and said, "Well I couldn't find any faults at all, and you would definitely have passed!" He sounded more chuffed with himself than me.

"Thanks, Kenny," I said trying to sound as downhearted as possible.

"What's wrong? I thought you would be pleased."

"I am, it's just I found out something awful this week and it's playing on my mind." I did my best to pretend to wipe away a tear, and looked away from him and out the window taking in a deep shuddery breath. After a moment, Kenny couldn't stand the silence and probed a bit deeper.

"What is it? Do you want to tell me? Perhaps I can help."

I waited for another ten seconds of torturous silence before giving another snippet of information, with sniffles in between the words, "It's…it's…oh, I don't want to burden you…it's just that you know of course my dad is disabled…and well, I found out that the manager who is meant to be running his business for him is actually cheating him!"

"Cheating him! How?" Kenny looked cross to hear my information. It seemed that despite his sleazy interest in young girls, he wasn't the kind of person to think it was okay that a disabled person was being taken advantage of.

"Well, I clean in the business sometimes, and I have suspected him for a while, but this week I overheard Richard – he's the manager – offering to take some of the customer's payment in cash. I think he has been doing this for months and I know for a fact the business is in terrible financial trouble, so working things out I suspect Richard is somehow stealing the company's money!" I always think when you are telling a story that to keep as close to the truth as possible makes it much more believable.

"That's terrible – why don't you tell your dad?"

"He relies completely on Richard and would be devastated to discover he was cheating him. I need to find a way of getting rid of him without upsetting my dad. I have come up with a plan of how to catch him out but I really need help from someone willing to pretend to be a customer…I did wonder if you would help but…but I feel awful asking you now, after everything you have already done for me." I started to sniffle again and rummaged in my bag for a tissue.

"Tell me, how would that work exactly?" It sounded like he was thinking about it.

"Well, whenever a customer is thinking about buying a car, Richard produces a printed quote for them to take away for consideration, and as you are a driving instructor, you could easily say you were thinking of purchasing a new car to set up your own business. In addition to the printed note we would need to record him offering you the cash part of the deal." I reached into my bag again and brought out a tiny Dictaphone. It had been given to Bill for Christmas one year and he had never used it, and it had ended up shoved in the back of a kitchen drawer. "If you had this in your pocket then we could catch him!"

Kenny looked a bit unsure about this plan and noticeably shifted in his seat. He was going to need more persuasion. I turned to face him and reached a hand up to the side of his face. "Just imagine if you did this how grateful I would be. You would be my hero, and next week in our *'lesson'* we could really celebrate." I leaned in and gave him a small gentle kiss on the cheek.

He shifted in his seat again. "Well, I guess it wouldn't be difficult for me to just pretend to be interested in buying a car…go on then, give me that Dictaphone; let's get the bastard!"

I didn't hear anything else from Kenny until the day before our final appointment. He telephoned the house, talking in code as if the small undercover job I had asked him to do had somehow made him into a detective. "I've got everything you need. Instead of me picking you up, meet me at my house in town this week; my address is on your lesson bookings sheet. Let's make it 6pm. I'm looking forward to it." Then he hung up before I could object.

Oh God, he wanted me to go to his house. This was not good. At least in the car there was always a door to escape from. How far would I go to get the evidence I needed to bring Richard down? I was going to have to go prepared for anything. Bill had pretty much stopped going to work at all now, so I hadn't been up to the garage cleaning either. Richard could be up to anything by now, completely left to his own devices. I really hoped Kenny had managed to get some incriminating evidence, and make this whole charade worthwhile.

That evening I waited for Ava to go and help Bill get ready for bed. Then I went to the medicine cupboard in the cat room. As Bill was now on various types of regular medication, I hadn't been asked to fetch any pills for some time as Ava just took him his cocktail of drugs with his food. I opened the door; there were stacks of bottles and boxes of drugs. I looked at a few of the containers; they all had weird long names and labels with Bill's name on. Then I spotted a box with Ava's name on it. This one was called Valium. Now that I had heard of. Why had Ava been prescribed it? I read the label: 'TAKE ONE AS DIRECTED. WARNING: THIS MEDICINE CAN CAUSE DROWSINESS, DO NOT EXCEED THE STATED DOSE'. Perfect, just what I needed. I opened the box; there were three sachets inside, each with eight little pills waiting to calm Ava's nerves. I took a whole new strip out, hoping it would be less likely to be noticed than just popping out a few pills. I replaced the box and went up to my room.

The pills were minuscule. If the dose to calm you down was just one then I guessed to knock someone out but not harm them would be four, or maybe six, just to be sure. I popped them out onto a clean piece of paper, then ground them into dust with the back of a spoon. I created a tiny paper envelope to house the toxin. There was my first defence.

Next I went back to the kitchen and took one of the sharp knives and a spray bleach cleaner from the utility room. Whilst in there I saw one of Ava's skimpy nighties on the wash pile. I might need that too, I thought, and stashed it as well. Finally, I visited the drinks cupboard and took out a brand-new bottle of brandy that Bill had been given by a client some years ago but had never opened. I packed the items into my rucksack; my precautionary weapons were ready. I really hoped I wouldn't have to use them.

The next morning while I was having breakfast Shawn came in. I didn't see him as much anymore as he had started university in the city and only sometimes came home at the weekend. "How's Carlos?" I ventured.

"Yea cool. We are officially dating now," he said chirpily before quickly adding, "Oh, don't mention that to Mum though."

"No worries. I don't suppose you could give me a lift into town later, could you? Around six? Just for old time's sake. I have my driving test next week so won't need any more lifts soon."

"Yea, I can do as I'm meeting Carlos in The Old Trout, but if you want a lift back you will have to come and find me in there, okay?"

"Sure, will do – thanks."

That afternoon I finished getting ready. This time I opted for tight jeans, a jumper and trainers, trying to make any access as difficult as possible. I put the little envelope of Valium in my pocket and carried the other 'weapons' in my rucksack. Shawn dropped me off in town and I made my way to Kenny's address. It was a Victorian mid-terraced house with cars parked all along the pavement. I felt sick with nerves. At six I rang the doorbell. Kenny opened it almost immediately, his smile slightly dropping when he saw my attire. "Come in! I've got something to show you that I think you might like."

I followed him inside and he closed the door behind me. I made a mental note of how his door worked in case of a rapid escape. He slipped past me and leapt up the stairs. "Follow me," he ordered.

We went into his bedroom. The bed looked like it had been cleanly made with the duvet neatly folded back. Across the middle a towel had been placed ready to catch my virginity. Presumptuous bastard.

"Now you sit down here while I show you what I have got." He sat me down on the edge of the bed then went to retrieve a leather case off the top of some drawers before sitting next to me. He slowly pulled out the printed quote and held it up for me to look at. Then he brought out the Dictaphone and suggestively pressed play, all the time focussed on my expression.

The bit of the recording he played featured him in conversation with Richard. They had clearly been chatting for some time, but then I heard Richard actually say, *'there's nothing illegal to worry about; it's simply a way for you to avoid some extra costs by paying me the deposit in cash.'* Kenny stopped the recording. "We got him! It felt so good, I felt like a secret agent!" He was as animated as a little boy who had just had a ride on a merry-go-round for the first time.

"Oh Kenny! You are so clever; thank you." I reached out to take the Dictaphone from him, but he withdrew it and placed it back inside the case with the quote. "You can have it after your lesson," he said with rather a chilling undertone.

He slid the case under the bed. I reached inside my bag and brought out the bottle of brandy. "I brought this for you; I thought it might relax us a little. Why don't you lie back and I'll just fetch us a couple of glasses from the kitchen?" I said with as much conviction as I could muster. I got up with the bottle and turned in the doorway to give him a little wink before heading downstairs to find some glasses.

Once in the kitchen I grabbed whatever glasses came to hand and poured a glug of brandy into each. I reached into my pocket and tipped the powdered Valium into one of the glasses. My hands were shaking so much, I could hardly tip it in without spilling any. I grabbed a spoon off the draining board and stirred up my potion. I heard Kenny call from above. I stuffed the bottle under one arm and went back up to the room, provocatively handing him the laced glass. "Cheers," I said. "A toast to you!" and I knocked back my drink in one. Kenny looked thrilled and mimicked me by also swallowing his drink in one. I opened the bottle to pour him another, but he took it from me and placed it on the bedside table. "Enough for now; let's get down to business."

"That leads me onto your second treat!" I said, pulling away and reaching back into my bag. I slowly pulled out Ava's silky nightie. "Where's your bathroom? I'll go and put this on for you."

Kenny's eyes nearly popped out his head; he obviously couldn't believe his luck. "It's just across the landing. Hurry up! I'm not sure how long I can contain myself," he said as he started pulling off his clothes.

I locked myself in the bathroom and sat on the edge of the bath taking a few deep breaths, and trying to calm myself down, praying for the Valium to kick in soon.

"What's taking you so long?" Kenny called after a few minutes. His voice sounded all woozy, like he was extremely drunk. The Valium was taking effect; I just needed to hold out a bit longer. After a few more minutes I heard some groaning. I slowly unlocked the door and peeped out – nothing. I crept back across the landing to the bedroom and peered inside. Kenny was lying naked face down across the bed, one arm dangling on the floor. He wasn't completely out yet as he was making little grunting noises. I ventured nearer the bed. His eyes were closed, and he was drooling a bit but hardly moving. I took his glass and rinsed it out in the bathroom. I also emptied half the bottle of brandy down the sink before pouring a little back in both glasses and placing one on each of the bedside tables. Next I ruffled up the duvet. I wanted him to think we'd had a wonderful time when he woke up, and to just put his lack of memory down to too much alcohol. I put the quote and Dictaphone in my rucksack then stood back to survey the scene. I noticed the towel still in the middle of the bed; Kenny had one leg draped over it. To make this completely believable, I needed some blood. I took the kitchen knife I had brought as protection and made a cut down my arm. I dripped some bright red blood onto the towel. There! Kenny was sleeping now and the scene was ready for him to wake up to. I left the house in disbelief that I had managed to escape unadulterated, and walked briskly into town without looking back.

I headed for The Old Trout to look for Shawn, eventually locating him in a window cubicle sitting on the same side and close up next to Carlos. "Hey."

Shawn sat up straight. "Hey. Er Carlos, this is my sister, Cathy."

"Good to meet you," Carlos said politely. I could immediately see why Shawn found him attractive. He had smooth, thick blonde hair – perfectly coiffed – clean, fresh skin, with a shaven chiselled jaw and his clothes looked immaculate – and expensive.

"You too." I sat down opposite them. The adrenaline was pumping through me still and I was breathing heavily.

"Are you okay?" Shawn asked.

I so desperately needed to tell someone about the evidence I had acquired that, without giving myself time to think, I started to tell them what I knew about Richard. I told them about the computer files I had on the floppy disk and I played them the recording Kenny had made – I pulled myself together enough not to mention how I had obtained the recording, and simply said my source didn't want to be identified. I told them I suspected Charles was involved as well and again omitted the part about Ava's infidelity, but told them all about his part and his father, Jack's, in ABC Cars, and the denial about the whereabouts of Bill's money.

When I had finished they both stared at me until eventually Shawn spoke, "I can't believe you didn't tell me all this sooner."

Carlos, who was in his final year of studying law, simply asked, "Why didn't you just go to the police?"

I glanced at Shawn. He knew about at least some of the dodgy business Bill had been involved with over the years to understand why going to the police was out of the question, but he didn't know about the Bugatti saga. If Shawn had been on his own I might have told him but involving Carlos was another matter. He must have read my mind because he said, "You can trust Carlos, and he won't betray your confidence, I promise. I can understand why greedy Charles is keeping the money for himself, but why would Richard do such a thing to Bill? They have been friends for years; why would he steal from right under his friend's nose like this?"

"All I can say is that Richard secretly hates Bill. What he is doing is revenge for something he believes is Bill's fault, which I know was not. Bill was simply trying to protect his family."

Carlos sat back in his seat with a look of deep concentration on his face. Shawn just looked bewildered. Eventually it was Carlos that spoke: "I am impressed at the great lengths you have gone to in order to obtain this recording."

"Evidence," I interrupted.

"Recording," Carlos repeated. "I'm sorry to be so blunt, but it would not stand up in a court of law and therefore cannot be used as evidence. The way you obtained it was entrapment, and I assume this unidentified source," he glanced down at the quote again, "or 'Kenny', doesn't know the full facts about why he was required to perform such an underhand job or indeed if he was even 'paid' for his work." Carlos stopped just long enough to give me a hard stare like my head teacher at school used to do when she was right and I was wrong, before he continued, "If what you say is true, and neither Bill nor Richard can go to the authorities, then there is nothing else within the law you can do."

"I'm not looking for an answer *within the law*," I said, mimicking Carlos. "I want to take my recording and threaten Richard with it." I was feeling angry now and was beginning to wish I hadn't told them. The lengths I had gone to and weeks of preparation I had made in order to obtain this recording, and Carlos just seemed to be rubbishing it.

Carlos noticed my irritation and calmly said, "I'm not saying there is nothing else *you* can do; I'm simply saying there is nothing else *within the law* you can do." He gave a wry little smile at the last bit.

"So what do you suggest? I need to get that money back from that thieving Charles, and stop Richard before he bankrupts the business and ruins us all."

"So – correct me if I am wrong – these are the facts and figures. One: Bill gave Charles' father Jack the excess profits from the business over several years – in cash –

amounting to around four hundred thousand pounds, which Charles now has. Two: Richard has been stealing cash payments owed to the business and, according to the spreadsheets you have seen, amounting to the region of one hundred and eighty thousand pounds."

When he put it in these terms, it really was an astonishing sum of money. "Yes – and it's probably a lot more than that by now."

"Cash is very difficult to dispose of – you can't just stick it in the bank."

Shawn and I sat in silence waiting for some kind of proclamation to come from Carlos.

"There's no way they could have cleaned hundreds of thousands of pounds in such a short time, so I would take an educated guess that they are stashing it somewhere."

"And we just need to find it!" I exclaimed.

"How are we going to find out where? We can't just follow them everywhere hoping they will pay a visit to their pension!" Shawn mocked.

Carlos sat back, looking thoughtful again, and after what seemed like an eternity he spoke. "Can you trust this Kenny?"

"Kenny? He's not completely furnished with everything, as I've just told you. All he knows is that Richard was stealing from Bill, and I needed his help to get some proof."

"Perfect," replied Carlos. "Will he do you another favour?"

My mind drifted to the position I'd left Kenny in about an hour earlier. I didn't know yet how he was going to react when – or if – he woke up. "Sure," I said anyway, keen to hear Carlos' plan.

"We need him to take the £2000 cash Richard asked for on the recording into the showroom and hand it over, telling Richard he'll go ahead with the deal."

This was hilarious! I started uncontrollably laughing.

"What's so funny?" Carlos demanded. He was not laughing. "Once Kenny has given Richard the cash, we can follow him, and see where he hides it."

I stopped laughing. "To start with, where exactly are we going to get £2000 in cash?!"

Now it was Carlos' turn to laugh. "Is that what you find funny?" He pulled his wallet out of his pocket and held it open on the table, so I could see inside. In the notes section there were about seven or eight £50 notes, several £20s and a £5. "Don't worry about the two grand; I can sport you that. You just need to persuade your friend Kenny to hand it to Richard."

I had to admit, this was quite a plan. Carlos had come up with a way to find out where the cash might be. My mind started to race ahead. "Once we know where the money is we can steal it back! Richard won't know it was us – maybe he'll even blame Charles – and with a bit of luck they will blame each other!"

"Slow down," Carlos said. "I think the first person they will blame might be Kenny. Is that his real name and address on the quote?"

I looked at it properly for the first time. In all the madness, I hadn't registered such minor details. "No, ha! He didn't use his real particulars! Clever bastard. I've just been at his house and it's only round the corner from here, not in Surrey!"

"You've been at this man's house?" Shawn interjected. "Who exactly is this man and how do you know him?"

"Oh don't get all protective! I can handle myself; don't you worry, big bro!"

Shawn looked deflated. "I'm going to get some more drinks in."

"Get me a pint!" I grinned.

"No!" Carlos barked.

"Are you for real? What we have just been discussing is highly illegal. I think buying an underage person a pint pales into insignificance," I scoffed.

"The difference is you could get caught and get Shawn in trouble right here and now in this pub. What we are talking about needs to be so watertight no one ever gets caught."

CHAPTER 19

Two days later, Shawn gave me an envelope with two thousand pounds inside from Carlos. I couldn't quite believe why he was so casual about that amount of money. He might never see it again. Shawn assured me Carlos could spare it and just wanted to help us to get justice for Bill. It was my turn next to convince Kenny to give it to Richard. My driving test would be the next day, so I assumed I would see him then, although I hadn't heard anything since leaving him sprawled on his bed Saturday night. I didn't dare call, so I arranged for Ava to drop me off at the test centre. She had been incredibly quiet since Charles had made his announcement the day I caught them together. She continued to carry out her duties and care for Bill, but rather than in her previous robotic and matter-of-fact way, she now appeared morose and melancholic as she cooked and washed. All her social activities had completely stopped, and even her appearance, which she had always taken so much pride in, had given way entirely to tracksuit bottoms and sweaters.

Bill also seemed more depressed than ever. He ate his meals in his room and refused to see the physio any more.

The house was beginning to look shabby and had a chill about it – not only that the heating was never on because of the expense, but the atmosphere had an inhospitable and forlorn air to it. A pile of mail and several red letters lay next to the door mat where no one had bothered to pick them up, signifying the inevitable doom that was coming. I just hoped I could find the money before it was too late and the debt engulfed us all.

Ava and I hardly spoke all the way to the test centre. I drove her car and she sat in silence simply murmuring 'good luck' as she got out and said she would go for a walk and meet me in an hour. I looked around for Kenny. He wasn't there. Why hadn't he come to support me? Perhaps he had realised I had drugged him. I ventured inside alone and filled out the relevant paperwork. My examiner was a stern looking middle-aged woman with a double chin and a giant mole on her neck. The first thing I said was to compliment her on her lovely suit. It's always best to win someone over with praise, I find. I did the test without any problems, and at the end I was duly passed. I should have been delighted, but with everything else on my mind it just didn't seem important any more. I clutched my certificate and waited for Ava by the car. I was standing there in the cold when a voice from behind me made me jump.

"Congratulations."

It was Kenny, looking incredibly sheepish. I was actually quite relieved to see him – at least it meant I hadn't killed him!

"I, er…just wanted to apologise…if, I…if I did anything I shouldn't have the other evening," he finally got out. "I just can't remember what happened and when I finally woke up you were gone."

At least my plan seemed to have convinced him. I looked down trying to appear hurt. "It's okay, Kenny. Afterwards, as you were sleeping, I used your phone to call my brother to pick me up and then I let myself out; I hope that was okay. I didn't feel very well; I think maybe that brandy was off or something and I just wanted to go home."

"Yes, yes of course, and you took the recording I noticed – was it useful?"

He was definitely feeling guilty now and he looked a bit worried as well. Now was my chance to push my luck.

"I have to confess, Kenny, that you acquiring that recording was great, and I tried to tell my dad about what Richard was doing, but he said in order for him to prove it he actually needs to catch him red-handed. So can I ask one more favour of you?" I reached into my bag and took out the envelope of cash. "Will you go back in and tell Richard you will go ahead with the deal and give him this money?"

Kenny looked inside the envelope, before pushing it back into my hands. "No, I don't think I should get involved any more – sorry."

"Oh Kenny, why?" I did my best to look disappointed. "All you have to do is give Richard the money, tell him you will do the deal and leave. After you have gone, Richard will be found out and that will be the end of it."

"I just don't feel comfortable with it."

It was time to play hard ball. "Well, I can't say I feel completely comfortable after what you did to me the other night. I haven't mentioned it to anyone yet, but now my brother knows where you live, I don't think he would need much persuasion to come round and see you, especially after he saw the state I was in."

Kenny looked surprised to see this other side of me, but came to his senses quick enough and snatched the envelope back. "Okay. Well, it would be easy enough just to call in and hand this over I suppose. I'm off tomorrow afternoon; I'll do it then. After this I don't think there will be any need for us to meet again."

I didn't want to risk him just keeping the money so threw in this last threat: "Agreed, and by the way, until you have handed over the money, you are being watched."

Ava ambled up just then and we got into the car leaving Kenny with two thousand pounds and a look of dismay.

She saw the smile on my face. "Just as well you passed. There is a surprise for you at home."

When we pulled in the drive, I saw it – the burgundy Morris Minor I had asked Bill for. I didn't expect to see it again, let alone all polished up and ready to drive!

"Paulo did a good job," Ava said. "He's a good chap; such a shame he's lost his job now."

"Why has he lost his job? He's the only mechanic left now, surely?" I exclaimed.

"Richard has decided to close the mechanics' area in order to make further cuts and one last attempt to save the business," Ava replied. "You were just lucky that Bill managed to retrieve this car out of the place before Richard sold it."

"Thanks," I said. It felt awful to know what Richard was doing and not be able to say anything. Just one more day, I told myself, then I'll catch him and sort this mess out.

I told Shawn about the plan for Kenny to seal the deal with Richard. He said he could pick me up after school with Carlos, so we could follow Richard after work. I took some home clothes with me to school to change into in the back of the car later. My school uniform was quite conspicuous and I didn't want anything to get in the way of catching Richard. Carlos and Shawn were waiting as planned. Carlos was driving so his car wouldn't be recognised. We drove over to the showroom and parked opposite in a side road. We could just about see Richard's parked car from our position. The business closed at 5pm but at 4:45pm we saw Richard start closing up. At five on the dot the lights were out and we saw Richard get into his car to leave.

"Come on! Start the engine," I urged Carlos. "We mustn't lose him now."

"Keep cool," Carlos said as he slowly pulled out and began tailing Richard. "We cannot risk him seeing us; we will only have one shot at this."

I really hoped Richard would lead us to his vault. I didn't know what we would do if he just drove home. We followed him for about twenty minutes – he didn't go home. He pulled down a cul-de-sac called 'Barney's Close'.

"Where are we?" I asked. "Who lives here?"

Shawn, who had been suspiciously quiet up to this point, perked up. "I recognise this place! I've been here before, years ago. Oh why was it now? Ah yes, I remember. I was with Bill…we called in here to see Jack."

Richard stopped outside number 35. Shawn and I ducked down inside the car as Carlos drove past and turned the corner, parking just out of sight. "Wait here," he instructed as he got out the car and gingerly peered back around the corner. After a few seconds he signalled us to follow and we hid behind him straining to see what was happening. Richard was waiting at the front door. An old woman answered; it was Jack's wife, Sal. They exchanged a few words then Richard gave her an envelope before turning to leave. We all dived out of sight and ran back to the car.

"Mission accomplished, I would say," announced Carlos. "Now we know two things for sure – one: Sal is involved and I would bet Charles is too. And two: the money is in that house."

"What now?" Shawn asked.

"Now we just need to plan what to do next," Carlos said.

Shawn went quiet again. I could tell he was considering how far he was prepared to go. He wasn't really one for breaking rules, and this job was definitely going to breach several. I didn't want to get anyone into trouble. Carlos had a bright future ahead of him, and he had already helped us enough. "Leave it to me. I'll find it and I promise to give you your money back first, Carlos. Thanks for all your assistance but you need to stay out of it from now on. You too, Shawn. We can't all risk getting caught."

Carlos drove us home. We didn't speak, all trying to find our own answer to the next phase, which basically meant breaking and entering. Just before I got out the car I said, "Thanks again, Carlos; see you soon I hope."

He tentatively said, "Let's meet on Sunday at mine. We can discuss ideas of how to move forward."

"Okay." I left the boys and went inside. Sunday was just three days away. I really didn't want to involve them anymore. I would have to come up with a plan and execute it before then.

Once inside the house I heard sobbing coming from the lounge. I peeped through the gap in the door; Ava and Bill were inside. Ava was dabbing her face with a tissue. "I can't stay, Bill. You must understand it's for the best. I don't blame you of course, but without me here you will be able to get the proper care you need. Once the debts are paid and the business is seized and the house is sold there will be nothing left, and the state will have to pay for your care. I'm young enough to start again. Let me go; don't steal these last few years from me as well."

"What about the kids?"

"Oh Bill, I have a son who has basically moved out and spends most of his time with his friends, and a daughter who can't stand the sight of me. I don't think I will be missed one bit."

Talk about hitting a man when he's at his lowest. I couldn't believe what she was saying: leaving us all to save herself. If I didn't hate her before I certainly did now. Well, let her go, I thought, let her go. I'll get the money back, and she won't see a penny of it. Fuck her.

I stormed up the stairs to my room not caring if they heard me, half hoping they did.

I had a terrible night. Intermittent dreams mingled with thoughts of how to steal the money, with a continuous thread of the conversation I had overheard running through everything. By morning, I only knew one thing for sure, and that was that getting the money was my priority. I would need to do whatever it took to get it back and save this family. My plan was pretty basic, but it might just work. After school, I gathered the things I would need: some latex gloves and a selection of tools from the garage. I copied Jack and Sal's phone number from the address book kept beside the phone, and I sorted out my black jeans, a dark blue hoodie and a scarf to use as a face mask.

Shawn was staying at uni again until the weekend so Bill, Ava and I ate dinner together for once. It was a sombre affair. I glanced up at Bill. "Thanks for the car, it's amazing. I'm taking it over to Layla's tonight."

"Good," was all Bill could manage; he hardly even looked up from his food that he had been pushing around the plate for the last ten minutes. "I think I'll go for a lie down; I'm not feeling great." And with that he wheeled himself out of the kitchen. Ava's eyes flicked up as he passed her, but she didn't object. Not wanting to be left alone with Ava, I got up as well.

"You won't mind if I skip the washing-up so I can get ready to meet Layla, will you?" Without waiting for a response I left. I couldn't let my anger for her interrupt my concentration for the job I was about to perform. I needed to keep my head and strategically focus on my plan.

Once back in my room I looked outside; it was almost eight and pitch black. I changed into my dark clothes and collected my prepared rucksack and keys, leaving the house quietly without any goodbyes. I drove to Barney's Close; the road was silent. The development consisted mostly of detached modern houses, all with a neat square of front lawn and a driveway leading to a garage. Only slight alterations distinguished one house from another – a hedge around the lawn or a brightly coloured front door. Most had some lights on inside and I imagined happy families behind the closed doors, sitting in comfort drinking cocoa and watching Friday night games shows.

As I cruised past number 35, I noticed a light on inside behind the drawn curtains and a single car parked on the drive. Sal would probably be sitting in front of the TV by this time, possibly dozing a bit. I parked my car in the shadows a couple of streets away, put on my rucksack and gloves and looked around to check if anyone was about. When I was confident the coast was clear I got out the car and headed for a phone box. I'd spotted one when we had followed Richard here the previous day. I put in 50p and dialled Jack and Sal's number. It rang three times before Sal picked up.

"Hello."

"Good evening. This is Nurse Donovan calling from the Ascot General Hospital. Could I speak with Mrs Sally Pincer please?"

"Yes, speaking."

"Are you the mother of Charles Pincer?"

"Yes, why? What's happened?"

"There has been a road traffic accident, and your son Charles has been involved. He is here in intensive care, and we would like you to come in straight away."

"Oh my…my Charles! Oh goodness, is he all right?"

"I'm sorry but I can't give you any further details over the telephone. The doctor will speak with you as soon as you get here. When you arrive, park in car park B and come straight to the desk at the Accident and Emergency entrance; it's clearly signposted."

"Yes, yes, I'm coming now."

I hung up the phone and checked the time on my watch. The hospital was a fifteen-minute drive away from here, so I deduced that I would have half an hour once Sal had left the house before she would return from the hospital, confused at the mix-up. I ran quickly, trying to stick to the shadows until I reached the corner nearest to number 35. Sal was just leaving the house and fumbling for her car keys. I knew it was cruel to trick an old lady like this but since it had become clear she knew at least some of what was going on, I put her in the same category as Richard and her son Charles. As she sped away down Barney's Close and towards the main road I crossed the street and disappeared behind her garage.

The garden was accessed through a half picket gate, so I was quickly out of sight and at the rear of her property. I'd hoped in her rush she might not have locked up properly and tried the back door handle. It stood firm. I looked along to see if any windows were ajar, then I noticed there was a conservatory added on the far side. I lifted the catch and tried the door which simply slid open smoothly for me; I was in.

The house was typically decorated for inhabitants of their age: flowery wallpaper and wall lights, highly polished mahogany tables with lacy doilies adorned with family photos in silver frames. To business, I thought. Where would you hide cash in a house like this? First I checked the layout of the house, aiming to search the study first. I went through the kitchen and lounge and located the study on the other side of the house at the bottom of the stairs. I went in. It was too dark to see but I didn't want to put a light on and draw attention to the house. In a location like this I could imagine a few curtain twitchers were out there. I got the torch from my rucksack and shone it around the room. A big old desk was the dominant feature with a wingback chair facing it. I rummaged across the desk contents before restraining myself. I mustn't get bogged down with looking for the wrong thing. The money wouldn't be on the desk! I shone the light towards a large filing cabinet with deep metal drawers. I opened one; it was stacked with files. I closed that one and opened the others quickly glancing in. It was the bottom drawer's contents that made me stop. The files in that one had labels attached at the top and the one that immediately caught my eye was ABC Cars. I flicked it open. There were columns filled in by hand across the page: dates, amounts and names, and the last entry at the very top said 'Richard £2000'. This was a record of the cash sums Charles had been collecting. I flicked to pages further back in the file and found Bill's name, again with the date and amounts listed. The file went back years, all neatly laid out, page after page. I noticed the handwriting changed after Jack's death, so someone – either Charles or

Sal – took over then, I guessed. It also looked like Richard had been conned into the same promise of investment that Bill had been and that was why he was giving the cash to Charles and Sal. I slipped the file inside my jacket and looked at my watch. Fourteen minutes had passed already and I needed to move quicker.

I began ransacking the downstairs rooms, desperately searching for a stash of money. Nothing. I flew up the stairs and started in the bedrooms. Flinging Sal's lifetime possessions around like confetti, I went through the wardrobes and checked the mattresses and bedding – nothing. Time would be getting short and I felt desperate. I went into the master bedroom. It was at the front of the house and some light from the moon shone in. I ripped off the bedding and pulled out the dresser drawers, manically searching for a sign – it could be anywhere: under a floorboard, in the loft, the garden shed even. I wasn't going to have enough time to look everywhere. I slumped to my knees, head in hands and a tiny glint just from under the bed caught my eye. I dived across and reached under. It was the metal catch on a suitcase. I slid it out from under the bed and clicked open the catches. Inside were bundles of notes, wrapped in equal sized packages in what looked like cling film. The case was packed full of them. I'd found the money!

Suddenly I was aware of a noise outside – it was the sound of an engine rumbling down the Close. I stood up to see a silver Jaguar turning up the drive; Charles' Jaguar. Sal must have called him from the hospital. Shit! I fastened the catches on the case and went to pick it up – it was so heavy, but adrenaline kicked in and I dragged it to the top of the stairs and pushed it down. It slid to the bottom with a thud. I lunged after it and hauled it back through the house to the conservatory. I heard a key in the front door now, and with a final urgency I lifted the case and disappeared into the garden, back the way I had come. I sprinted across the street making a scraping noise as I dragged the case on the ground behind me. I didn't care if anyone saw me now – I just simply had to make it back to my car. As I veered around the corner I heard a door open but I didn't turn to look, I just kept forcing the case towards my parked car. I thrust it across the back seats and jumped in the front, started the engine and propelled the car into action, not thinking where I was going, just speeding away from there.

I drove for at least ten minutes, constantly looking in my rear-view mirror, but wasn't aware of being followed by a silver Jag. My heart was beating so fast I could hardly breathe. My back felt awkward where I was still carrying my rucksack, and my hands were sweating in the latex gloves and shaking from the effort of carrying the weight of the case. I turned to glance in the back of the car, to check it really was there. Then the realisation of what I had done hit me, and I started to laugh. I laughed so hard that tears started pouring down my face and I could hardly see. I pulled into a lay-by and switched off the engine. I didn't know if Charles had seen me or not but for this moment in time I had won and it was his turn to suffer.

CHAPTER 20

After tortuously thinking where to store the suitcase where it would be safe, I simply put it in the boot of my car. I would present it to Bill after Ava had left, which I assumed from her words the other evening would be very soon. I used the household copier to make photocopies of the most recent entries in the file and stashed them with the original and the floppy disk in my underwear drawer.

The day after my raid was Saturday. I had a long lie-in before heading downstairs in my pyjamas for breakfast. I stopped in the hall to look out at my Morris Minor, sitting there innocently on the drive ignorant to the crime it had been involved in. I smiled to myself, delighted to have beaten that crook Charles. The post unexpectedly got shoved through the door, landing on the mat and making me jump. I collected it up and put the letters one by one on the floor with all the other mail that had accumulated there.

At the bottom of the pile was a letter addressed to me. On the front of the envelope there was a stamp that read HM Prison Service. Inside was a Visitation Order form from Piper Avery. The form had been filled out by Piper herself requesting me to arrange to visit her in prison. How odd that after all this time she should want to see me. I read the information. It said that the recipient would need to bring ID; examples were a driving licence or passport and if under the age of eighteen, a guardian would be required to accompany the visitor. It listed the standard visiting times and explained to bring this form and the relevant ID during visiting hours. Poor Piper; I often thought of her. She must be used to prison by now, but I would like to know how she was coping. I still owed her for not involving me in the whole saga. There was no question that I would make the visit; I would get Shawn to accompany me.

Shortly after, Shawn called to let me know Carlos's address. We arranged to meet there at three the next day. Although I was desperate to share my news, I didn't mention the plunder; it could wait until I saw him. After breakfast, I slipped out to my car and opened the suitcase in the boot. I counted twenty-five bundles inside, each wrapped in cling film. They all appeared to be made up of £20 notes. I removed one bundle and took it up to my room to count, so I could get an estimate of how much I had actually taken. I unwrapped the cash and laid it out in small heaps of £1000 across my bedroom floor. I made a neat row of twenty little piles – £20,000. So stashed in my little car boot was half a million! About a hundred grand short according to my calculations of what Bill had lost, but I wasn't about to complain. I kept out £2000 to give back to Carlos then wrapped the rest and put it back in the suitcase in my car.

The next day I drove over to Carlos's house as planned. It was tricky to find and I was hoping he had a secure driveway I could park on. I felt nervous driving around with almost half a million pounds in my boot. Eventually I found his road on the edge of Woking. It was a long tree-lined avenue packed with parked cars. The only gaps were where there was an entrance to a house. I crawled along looking for one named 'Random Lodge', which took a couple of attempts driving up and down to find. I turned into the drive and spotted Shawn's car, so parked alongside. I locked my car and walked up to an enormous front door and rang the bell. Shortly after, I heard the door being unbolted and Carlos appeared.

"Welcome, my little felon!" he beamed giving me a warm hug and pulling me inside.

"Hey," I replied.

I followed him through a large tiled hallway to the rear of the house where Shawn was lounging on a sofa wearing just his T-shirt and boxers, and sipping a mug of tea. The house had a lovely homely atmosphere and once again I felt a little envy for Shawn having Carlos as a boyfriend.

"Tea?" Carlos asked.

"Yea, cool." I sat opposite Shawn while Carlos made fresh tea. The area we were in and the kitchen were open plan, and double doors led out onto a terrace at the back. It was gorgeous. "Is this your place?" I enquired.

"Ha, not yet!" he joked. "It's my parents' house, but they spend most of their time in the States now, so they have left me in residence while I finish my degree." He handed me a mug. "There you go."

"Thanks."

"So now, strategy time!" he announced. "Anyone come up with an idea of how to retrieve this stolen money?" He was clearly enjoying the drama of our family and was treating it almost like a game.

I left a dramatic pause for effect then said, "Actually, I have." Carlos and Shawn turned to look at me. I reached inside my bag and took out the £2000. "I believe this is yours," I declared and held out the money to Carlos.

"Where did you get that?" Shawn demanded, sitting up and snatching the cash. He started sifting through it and manically counting it out.

Carlos, who obviously had no need or care for the money, looked at me directly and with a grin on his face probed, "What have you been up to now, little Catty?"

I relayed my exploits to them, vividly describing how close I came to being caught. I omitted to mention the suitcase was actually sitting just a few metres away on the front drive though. Once I had finished, Carlos erupted into applause. Shawn, however, erupted in a different way.

He stood up and started ranting, "Are you insane?! What if you had been caught? Who knows what this lunatic is capable of? I can't believe you did this without telling us! What were you thinking?" He carried on pacing up and down until eventually he stopped, exasperated, and slumped back down in the sofa, head in hands.

"Chill," I said calmly. "He didn't catch me and I'm sitting here now absolutely fine. I know we planned to discuss this today, but I just couldn't risk you both getting involved any more. It had to be done, so I did it and that's that."

Carlos addressed me next. "You are really something. I must admit I am exceedingly impressed. Tell me, where's the money now?"

"Somewhere safe."

"Okay," Carlos nodded, and didn't press me for any more details. I was really beginning to like him.

"What are you going to do now?" Shawn started up again. "You can't just hand over all that cash to Dad! He will have questions, and you and I both know he will get the truth out of you."

"Shawn is right; you can't just hand it over. Even if we came up with a good story and persuaded Bill to accept it, what could he do with the money now? He can't save his business – Richard would be suspicious and Charles certainly would. We need to keep quiet and hope Charles will suspect Richard is behind this. He can't exactly go to the police and report his suitcase full of stolen cash has been taken, so I would assume he'll take the law into his own hands."

"I agree," Shawn said. "Wait it out. I quite often find that doing nothing is the best thing to do."

"Of course you do," I said snidely, briefly returning to childhood rivalry before checking myself. Then I remembered the other thing I needed to ask. "On a slightly different tack, I have received this." I handed them the Visitation Request form from Piper and waited patiently while they read it.

"Why has she sent you this?" Shawn said looking miffed.

"Isn't this the person who was on trial when we first met in court?" Carlos asked Shawn.

"Yes it is. She was my art teacher, Piper Avery," I said. "She used to give me some extra tuition and we became friends. It was her first job at my school – she's only a bit older than you both. That was why I asked Shawn to follow the trial."

"You are full of surprises!" Carlos declared.

"It still seems odd that she would ask you to visit her in prison," Shawn said.

"Well anyway, as I'm under eighteen I need to be accompanied by a guardian, so will you come, Shawn?"

"Of course he will!" Carlos interrupted. "The chance to visit an inmate when you are studying law! I wish I could come!"

Shawn performed his usual ritual of remaining quiet to give the impression he was thinking before answering, "All right."

"Great, it says we can go on a Saturday. Can we go next week? You just need to bring your passport."

"Fine. The prison is nearer to here, so why don't you come over lunchtime and we can go on?"

"Okay, thanks." I took the letter back and stood up to leave. "Thanks, guys. It feels good to have shared all this with you."

I wasn't lying. As I drove back home I felt enormous relief: finally I wasn't alone any more. I had people on my side for a change, although I still kept some details about that night from them: I hadn't mentioned the file…

When I arrived back home, Richard's car was on the drive. I parked my car and went inside quietly. I stood in the hall and listened, trying to locate voices and determine which direction they were coming from. After a few seconds I just about made out some noise coming from Bill's bedroom at the end of the long corridor, so I crept in that direction, aware to keep an eye out behind me in case Ava appeared. The door was closed but I could hear voices now. Richard was speaking in a fairly animated way. "I'm convinced things will pick up, Bill. Don't close the business yet; I'll work harder for you, I promise."

"I'm sorry, Richard, I've already set it in motion. Bob has agreed to buy up the remaining stock and I've given notice on the tenancy. You know I'll do my best to put in a good word for you with the other dealers but I just can't employ you any more. I need to sort out my affairs while I still can, starting with closing the business down with immediate effect."

Richard had been too greedy. If he hadn't stolen quite so much money from the business, he could have kept his scam going for years. I did feel a bit sorry for him though. I had always liked him, and although he was stealing from my family, he was only trying to save his. I soundlessly tiptoed back up the corridor and up the stairs to my room. Locating the original file containing all the sums of cash Charles had recorded that I had taken from Sal's house, I slipped back downstairs and out to the drive. I tried the door handle of Richard's car; it opened. I stuffed the file under the passenger seat. I might not see Richard again and thought maybe he deserved to know the truth about Charles one day. Then just to make sure I wasn't there to raise any suspicion, I got back into my car and drove out to the woods to wait for Richard to leave.

CHAPTER 21

I had fundamentally hated my entire school career, and couldn't wait for it to finish, so I could get to art college. I had to rely on Mr Cartwright to help me achieve that dream now, and decided he was just about competent enough to get me accepted. I stayed behind working on my portfolio with him and a few other students every Wednesday. I didn't often speak in these sessions, but this time I asked him a question. "Did you see 'The Forcibly Bewitched' painting by Goya when we were on the school trip to The National Gallery, Mr Cartwright?"

"Oh yes, in the main hall. I remember hearing about that robbery on the news. They were lucky to find it; paintings that go missing are rarely found."

"Do you think the guy who owned the house where they found it paid a lot for it?"

"Oh millions, I'm sure! Really a work like that is priceless. Just imagine having a work by one of the Old Masters on your wall!"

Maybe not on the wall but hidden in a cupboard, I thought to myself.

"How do they know it isn't a forgery?" I dared to ask.

"I think the experts know the difference," he grinned back at me.

Obviously they bloody don't, I thought.

Mr Cartwright continued, "Although having said that, there was a very famous case in America a few years back where, following a theft, a museum recovered a painting and reinstated it in the collection only for the real one to turn up a year later! When questioned, the director of the museum admitted they knew it was a forgery, but it was so like the real one – and they didn't want to lose face – that they decided to put it on display for the public anyway!"

"So do you think The National Gallery might be doing the same thing?"

"Of course not. I don't have any doubt they have the original."

Maybe it didn't matter if they knew or not. Nicholas's copy was so good it deserved to be on display, and as the man they arrested was a criminal who would almost certainly have contacts that could trace down Ed and kill him for selling a forgery, maybe it was for the best anyway.

Bill, Ava and I were having dinner later that evening, all sitting in our customary silence as we ate. Ava had given up on her culinary health fad and started buying in frozen ready-meals now; tonight was beef and ale pie with peas. Suddenly the telephone broke the silence, making us jump and without moving we all looked at each other as if one of us would know who would be calling at this time. After a few seconds when no one stirred, Ava got up to answer it with a huff.

"Hello…Ah, April, hello what can we do for you at this time?…No…he came over last weekend but not since then, no, why?…Oh don't worry…Charles?…No…oh all right, well let me know when you hear and try not to worry."

She came back to the table. "How strange. That was April. She said Richard is missing."

"Missing?" Bill repeated.

"Yes, she said Charles came over to the house last night to talk to Richard, and he was in a strange mood. After a few minutes he started making so much commotion that April said he would wake Rosie, so she told them to go down the pub. So they left, and she hasn't heard from Richard since. Charles must have come back at some point because in the morning April noticed his car was gone, but Richard and his car are still missing."

"That's odd. What did Charles say about it?" Bill asked.

"Apparently she can't get hold of him either."

"I'm sure Richard just drank too much and is sleeping it off somewhere. He didn't take me telling him he was out of a job very well, what with his young family and everything, but I didn't have a choice. I'm sure he will be fine." Bill sounded more like he was trying to convince himself than Ava.

"Yes, well I've asked her to let us know when he turns up."

My mind began a train of thought. If Charles retrieved his car later, they must have gone to the pub in Richard's car. And if Charles sat in Richard's car, what if he saw the file I left under the passenger seat? He would recognise it straight away and accuse Richard of stealing the money. What did he do? Yell at him? Beat him? Kill him? No, surely Charles wasn't capable of such a thing, and anyway, Richard was innocent – well, of this anyway. Like Bill said, Richard will turn up…

But by the time the next weekend came around Richard hadn't turned up and on Saturday morning April came over with Rosie. Ava brought them into the lounge where Bill and I were sitting, and I played with Rosie pretending not to listen. "Any news?" Bill asked.

"No, nothing. I've been over to Charles' house but he's not there, and he's not answering his phone at home or work. I did speak to Sal, and she admitted to seeing him and tried to palm me off with some rubbish that he left Richard in the pub and got a taxi back to my house to collect his car. I don't believe a word of it. Why would he not tell me himself if he has nothing to hide?"

"That is very strange. Charles and Richard are good friends; he must be as concerned as you are. I'm sure he's just busy," Ava said, still loyally protecting Charles, I noted.

"Well you wouldn't have thought so if you saw him when he came over! He was extremely upset about something, I've never seen him so worked up. Oh, why did I send them out? If I hadn't Richard wouldn't be missing." April broke down and started sobbing.

"Have you reported this to the police?" Ava enquired.

"No, not yet." April glanced nervously at Bill.

"Maybe you could make us all some tea?" Bill told Ava in a tone she knew meant he needed privacy. Ava got up and left the room.

"Why not?" Bill directed at April.

"Look, Bill, we've all done things that we would rather the police didn't poke into but I can't just do nothing. I will have to involve them eventually; I need help to find Richard." April shifted around then got up. "I shouldn't have come. I just wanted to warn you, that's all." She bundled Rosie up in her arms to leave. "Sorry, Bill, we all want the same thing really, for the ones we love to be safe." And with that she left.

I stared after her, deep in thought. Maybe April knew that Richard had been fleecing Bill, but she clearly had no idea about how Charles was now deceiving Richard into handing over his spare cash in exactly the same way his father Jack had done to Bill. But if the police started investigating, who knew what they might find? They would certainly discover the dodgy accounting Richard had been up to and that would lead to all kinds of questions. Despite Richard's terrible betrayal of Bill, I really did hope he would turn up soon.

With the morning's commotion I had forgotten the time, and, glancing down at my watch, I realised it was noon. I needed to head over to Carlos's if I wanted to make it to the prison today.

When I arrived, Carlos had lunch on the table. "I thought we could have a quick bite to eat before heading off!" he declared as he presented me with a plate of his home-made coronation chicken salad. Shawn was already on his second portion. "You're lucky there's any left with this bottomless pit around!" he said ruffling Shawn's hair affectionately.

"Thanks," I said tucking in. I was hungry. After a few mouthfuls I announced, "Richard is missing."

"What?" Shawn asked looking up from his lunch.

"Apparently he had a row with Charles and hasn't been seen since."

"Well this is perfect news!" declared Carlos. "Charles must suspect Richard is the thief!"

"Yes, but what has he done to Richard? April said he was acting very weird. What if he's hurt him?"

"I thought you were tough. After what you have done, it's a bit late now to start showing compassion," Carlos said.

He was right. I hadn't even told him about the file and Carlos assumed I was basically to blame for whatever Charles had done to Richard. "Come on, we'd better get going," I said.

Shawn and me headed off to the HMP Holloway promising to relay everything about the place back to Carlos later. As we approached the prison I felt a chill; it was a huge site covered in faceless red brick buildings. We had to stop at a gate and show our ID before being directed to visitor parking, after which we made our way to the entrance, and once inside the smell of disinfectant was so strong I could hardly breathe. We shuffled along with other visitors through the security checks and into a locker room where we had to place all personal possessions until after our visit. Next we went through a metal detector, then finally were briefly frisked by a security guard and told to go and sit at a table to wait for our relevant inmate.

"It's quite exciting isn't it?" Shawn whispered as we waited.

I was anxiously looking about for Piper. Several other prisoners filed in, greeting their loved ones and sitting down at their table to talk. Then I saw her. She looked quite different to how I remembered. Her silky long dark hair now looked matted and frizzy, and although she was always very slim, now she looked malnourished and skinny. She was moving slowly like she was uncomfortable as she approached our table with a weak smile. "Thank you for coming."

I felt sick seeing her like this. Poor Piper. "Hi. This is my brother, Shawn."

"Hello," Shawn said. "I watched your trial. I'm very sorry about your circumstances." He sounded like he was at a funeral.

Piper gave him a kind look. "Thank you. Just over there, can you see the drinks machine, Shawn?" She pointed across the room. "Could you possibly get me a tea? I'd love a hot drink."

"Oh yes, of course." Shawn jumped up and went to the machine, where a small queue had begun to form.

I looked back at Piper. "I'm so sorry." I could feel the tears forming and clenched my teeth. "This is all my fault."

Piper looked earnestly at me across the table as she leaned in. "No. That's exactly why I asked you to come. I want to thank you. You saved me from a monster. I know how you helped…with the…" She glanced around, checking the guard wasn't within earshot. "…The white box," she whispered.

I looked down at the table and smiled, recalling how I had nearly been caught that day. "It was the least I could do after you didn't dob me in for the…" I mimicked her checking we weren't being overheard, "gun."

We both giggled and Shawn reappeared with the tea. Piper sat back up straight to sip her tea. "Thanks. It's lovely to have some visitors."

"Don't your family come?" Shawn blurted out thoughtlessly.

Piper looked upset again. "No, they don't come. No one comes. It gets very lonely."

"We'll come every week!" I announced.

Shawn glanced at me. "Yes, well maybe not every week but when we can."

"Don't worry. Next year once I'm eighteen I won't need a chaperone." I rolled my eyes at Shawn.

"Thanks. If you could come once a month, it would really give me something to look forward to," Piper said.

"We can definitely manage that, can't we, Shawn?" I gave him a piercing look.

"Yes, absolutely," Shawn confirmed, nodding.

We spent the next fifteen minutes chatting about the school and the replacement teacher Mr Cartwright. Piper gave me a few pointers on what to say in my upcoming interview for art school. Then a bell sounded signalling visiting was over, and we left promising to visit again in a month.

CHAPTER 22

Later in the week, Bill said the police had been round to question him. April had now reported Richard as missing, and they were looking into his recent behaviour. On hearing the news that Bill had just informed Richard he was out of a job, the police suspected Richard had just taken off for a while. They had managed to talk to Charles who also confirmed Richard had confided in him on that last evening how he was distraught about losing his job. That slime bag Charles could talk himself out of anything. What had he really done to poor Richard, and where was he now?

Friday was my interview in London for art school. I loaded my portfolio I had spent the last month preparing with Mr Cartwright into the back of my car and headed off for the city. The suitcase with half a million pounds still sat in the boot. I had thrown a couple of old blankets over it, but that was all I had done to hide it.

I found the college and headed in for my interview half an hour early. Two scruffy men introduced themselves as the heads of Art, Mike and Drew, and took me through to one of the studios. The interview was as casual as they looked. We joked and chatted, and they looked through my work with great enthusiasm. I felt right at home here: this was where I needed to be; I was in my element. After thirty minutes they offered me a place starting next September and that was that. A letter would arrive confirming my offer within a week. I was buzzing as I sped home unable to stop grinning. At last there was something to look forward to. I decided right then to give Bill the money. I would tell him everything and then it was up to him where he hid the cash, but I would be free to get on with my life without the burden of it.

When I pulled into the drive Ava's car wasn't there. It was an unusual time for her to be out; she would normally be preparing the dinner by now. Perfect for me though – I could tell Bill about the money right now. I burst into the house and poked my head into the lounge – Bill wasn't there. He must be in his room. I headed down the long corridor to check, but he wasn't there either. There weren't many more places he could be. I inspected the rest of the downstairs – the kitchen and bathroom – but he was nowhere to be found. He hardly ever went out any more but there was one last place to check; maybe he'd gone out in his car. I went to the carport, and as I approached I could see the car there, but the driver's door was open. As I went around the vehicle I saw the wheelchair on the ground on its side, and there next to it Bill was lying motionless.

"Dad!" I yelled and rushed over and crouched on the ground next to him. He had banged his head and there was some blood on his hair and the ground. His eyes were half open like he was semi-conscious. "What happened?

I'll go and call an ambulance." But as I went to stand up Bill tried to catch my arm and say something.

"Ch…Ch…"

I squatted back down and took his hand. "What is it?"

"Cha…Charles," he managed to whisper.

"Did Charles do this?" I looked urgently at him but all he could do was blink. Tears began to fall down my face now. "Oh God I'm so sorry! This is all my fault. I have the money Charles is looking for – do you hear me? I have the money!" I stood up and rushed inside to call an ambulance. After giving our location I ran back to Bill's side; he wasn't conscious now. "Dad!" I shouted at him. "Dad! Wake up! I have your money!" I shook his shoulders to try to wake him, make him understand it was all going to be okay now. "I have your money! I have your money!" He wasn't moving. I lay down next to him holding his hand and repeating the phrase over and over again, "I have your money."

Forty minutes later the paramedics arrived and he was pronounced dead.

Ava miraculously appeared as Bill was being loaded into the ambulance. "What's happening?" she cried. The paramedics told her the news. I was still sitting on the ground beside the pool of congealing blood. She turned to look at me. She genuinely seemed shocked to see me there. "What were you doing here?"

What a strange question. "I got back early. Where have you been?" I demanded.

"I just popped round to Kate's for a cup of tea and time just slipped away. Oh poor Bill; if only I'd been here."

She began weeping. "I warned him not to go out on his own."

"He wasn't on his own," I said coldly, now beginning to wonder about Ava's story. Kate was one of her old friends, but she hadn't mentioned her for months.

Ava completely ignored my statement and said to the paramedics, "His wheelchair must have slipped backwards trying to get into the car. He has lost a lot of strength recently." She broke down weeping again.

"We have informed the police as a matter of course. I suggest you both go inside and wait for them to arrive. We will take Bill to the hospital mortuary now," said one of the paramedics.

"Yes, of course. Thank you."

Ava leant down and linked her arm inside mine to lever me up and we went back inside the house. We made our way into the kitchen and I went to the sink to wash my face. There was dried blood on my hands. I don't remember it getting there and I rubbed it away, tears still falling and mingling with the tap water. My head was pounding. Ava was talking, but I couldn't hear her. Guilt and regret and questions filled my head but I couldn't speak. Eventually I switched the tap off and turned to face her. The police were there – I hadn't even heard them arrive.

A young female policewoman introduced herself. "My name is PC Jenny Hicks. I'm very sorry about your father. Do you feel up to telling me what happened?"

I needed to think but my head was a mess. "I came home to find him lying on the ground by his car."

"I know this is hard. Was he conscious at all when you found him?"

I looked over to Ava who I could feel was focussed on my every move. Why was she out when I came home? I glanced back at the PC, then flicked my gaze back to Ava. "Yes."

The PC also looked over at Ava, noting the connection. "And did he say anything?" she pushed.

Ava made a large wailing sound to distract the conversation. "Oh my poor Bill!" she sobbed, and the PC went to console her, leaving her last question hanging.

Her delay tactic gave me a few moments to think. If I mentioned Charles, what good would it do? There was no evidence he was even here let alone involved with forcing Bill to the ground. So Bill said his name; it meant nothing without a motive and to justify that, the police would need to know the whole truth. Anyway, he was bound to have an alibi set up already knowing him. But he wouldn't get away with this, I would make sure of that myself.

PC Hicks turned back to me, "So, did he say anything?"

"No."

CHAPTER 23

It wasn't long before Bill's death had been officially ruled as an accident. I had hardly said a word to Ava who had thrown herself into making the funeral arrangements. Shawn had come home briefly to see us, but Billie-Joe, who had permanently moved to Spain now, and Jane, still in Germany, had been told over the phone. Neither of them would come back to England for the funeral.

On Saturday I forced Shawn to take me to see Piper again. I needed to talk to someone about what had happened and she would want to know how my interview had gone. I asked Shawn to hang around by the drinks machine, so I could speak to Piper in private. The guards didn't seem to take any notice of us, just pacing the room watching all the other inmates and looking bored. I briefly explained to Piper that I suspected Charles had killed Bill, and possibly Richard, but without telling her the full facts, it was difficult for her to process.

Finally, she said, "The most important thing is that you keep safe. I have made a few contacts in here and I can give you the number for someone that can help you with this Charles character if you feel that is the way you need to take things."

She was being deliberately cryptic but I understood exactly what she meant. "Thanks, but I need to take care of Charles myself."

"Be careful; you don't want to end up in here with me!" she said with a warning tone.

Once outside the prison and back in the car with Shawn I had time to think. It had helped to see Piper. I reminded myself of the evidence I had accumulated: the floppy disk and the copy I had made of Charles' incriminating file. Now I just needed to think of the best way to use them.

Ava had invited just about everyone Bill knew to the funeral. She spent day after day on the phone receiving compassion from various acquaintances as she explained what had happened over and over again. The whole tragedy had given her a boost, and she was almost savouring the sympathy. Instead of wearing her drab wardrobe of recent months she dug out her flirty dresses once again, and entertained visitors to the house most evenings as she informed them of the funeral arrangements and absorbed their kindness.

The funeral had been booked for Friday at the crematorium, followed by a wake back at the house. I had taken the whole week off school and witnessed the gross and almost perverse way in which Ava was dealing with everything and everyone. I had given up listening in on her conversations until Thursday when Samuel Atkinson arrived for a meeting. He was Bill's solicitor and came with his assistant Carry – who only looked old enough to be on work experience – to explain the next steps to Ava.

"Before the official reading of the will I just wanted to give you a heads up, Ava. As I'm sure you are aware, Bill was having financial trouble. Fortunately he managed to tie up the business by signing a deal with Bob Fox so that is now off your hands. However, his personal accounts are pretty much empty and his only remaining asset was this house. I don't know if you were aware, but he recently made a new will that divides all his assets equally between you and the two children from his first marriage. Unless you have enough personal money to buy them out, this house will need to be sold straight away."

"What? I have to leave my own home? I thought his will said that I would inherit everything."

"The old one did, but after you told him you were going to leave him, he changed it."

"He told you that? I wasn't serious, I was just venting my frustration – have you any idea how difficult it is to care for someone twenty-four hours a day? Surely this new will can't be legal."

"It is. Unless you have the funds to contest it then there is nothing you can do, and as he had a previous family it is quite acceptable for him to have left them something, so I doubt you would be successful anyway. Your own children will inherit from you eventually as is the natural course. You can stay living here while the property is sold and you look for somewhere else to live. Then you can find yourself a nice little job. You're still young; you have plenty of good years' work left in you."

Samuel was clearly teasing Ava. Everyone knew she didn't want to work. She looked distraught; all that newly gained glow draining slowly from her face. "But, I don't understand. When did he change his will? He hadn't been out the house for weeks. Charles told me the house would be worth about a million. If half goes to Billie-Joe and Jane, how am I going to manage?"

"He made the arrangements with me over the phone and I popped over for him to sign the papers last week. I believe you were out shopping at the time. Why would Charles be interested in the property value?"

I knew the answer to that. Charles would clearly do anything to get his hands on Bill's fortune, including seducing Ava. "Oh it was just an observation he made," Ava said brushing her previous statement away.

"Well anyway, I just wanted to let you know. The estate agents will be in contact with you next week to make accurate valuations of the property for probate. I'll see you at the funeral tomorrow."

Samuel and his sidekick Carry got up to leave. I made myself disappear momentarily from my secret viewing position until they had left, then I shifted into the lounge to where Ava still sat motionless.

"What did they want?" I asked casually.

Ava looked up at me blankly. "I have to sell the house. I won't be able to afford anything around here, so I will have to move away."

"Well don't worry about me," I said sarcastically. "I'll be moving to London in September anyway. Oh, did I mention I've been offered a place at art college? As soon as my exams are done, I'll be out of your way."

"Well, you have always been independent, so I'm sure you will be fine." She hardly even looked at me, relieved perhaps that I was going anyway without needing a push, so embroiled in her own sense of disappointment it was palpable.

I left and went up to my room. I needed to make plans of my own. The mechanics of the house sale and probate would take about six months; time for me to finish my exams and sort out accommodation in the halls of residence. I could stay with Shawn for a few weeks if necessary. I was very aware of keeping the money in my car boot, but with agents and potential purchasers followed by surveyors visiting the house, I couldn't think of a safer place. Next I sorted out my outfit for the funeral. I owned quite a few black items from my Goth phase last year so it was quite an easy choice, but I felt it would take the stress out of thinking about it tomorrow. Finally, I located the copy of the file I had taken from Sal's house and the floppy disk containing Richard's dodgy accounts. I folded the paper up and placed it with the disk inside an envelope. Now Bill was gone there seemed little point in keeping this secret. The truth might lead the police to finding Richard and at least give April some answers.

The next morning I went down to breakfast. Shawn had already arrived; the three of us would travel in the car to the crematorium together. I sat down at the table but couldn't eat anything. Ava flounced in, already dressed in a tight black dress with patent black stilettos, her hair swept up in a bun with a few curls left dangling to soften her face. "I've cancelled the wake," she announced.

Shawn looked up perplexed. "Why?" he breathed.

"It was all costing too much, and half the guests hadn't RSVP'd so it has been impossible to cater for."

"I thought the caterers were already booked?"

"Well, I cancelled them yesterday."

Shawn looked at me expecting a response, but I knew the deed was done. What could I say now? I didn't really care. Most of Bill's so-called friends hadn't been round to visit him for months, so I never really understood why we should throw them a party anyway.

"The car will be here at ten; make sure you are both ready," she said before leaving the kitchen.

We arrived at the crematorium in silence. Ava hadn't shed a tear down her perfectly made up face. I could see Shawn was clenching his teeth, doing his best to appear strong and we shared a brief look of support towards each other. The rest of the gathering were already milling about the venue, a sea of black umbrellas hovering in the drizzle. Once outside the car, Ava began her role acknowledging the friends and relatives as we made our way behind the coffin and filed into the cold building. I kept my head down, just concentrating on the shuffling feet, not wanting to look at these fake sympathy givers. After we were seated some stranger said a few words, then Terry stood up to give a brief eulogy. I hardly took it in, tears were falling now and all my attention was focussed on my own sorrow.

The curtains closed as the coffin was mechanically moved into place signalling that the service was over and we could all leave. Ava got up and led the way out, Shawn and I trudging behind. Outside again, we walked along a corridor of wreaths that had been laid out for us to appreciate and thank people for. I moved away towards the cars feeling hands patting me on the shoulder and mumbling words of how sorry they were. Ava remained a while admiring the flowers and absorbing the attention one last time. April was close by her side, balling her eyes out as if this was her chance to mourn for Richard as well. Suddenly I became aware of someone in front of me handing me a clean tissue.

"I'm very sorry for your loss."

I recognised the arrogant, conceited voice straight away: it was Charles. He was standing there in his immaculate navy suit with his officious attitude and eternal slither of a grin. Before I had time to think I replied.

"And I am very sorry for yours." I looked him directly in the eye, blinking my tears back as hatred took over.

For the tiniest of seconds I saw his façade drop and his usual perfection replaced with a brief expression of alarm before quickly regaining control and saying, "What loss would that be?"

I regained my composure as well. I could play at his game too and diverting the meaning of my comment I said, "Well, of course it wasn't that long ago that you also lost your own father. I'm sure, being an accountant, he had all his affairs neatly sorted for you to simply step in and continue. Unlike Bill of course." I paused for effect. "I assume Ava filled you in on the changes he made to his will?"

He looked rattled again and glanced at the crowd which was now dispersing, searching for Ava. Clearly she was yet to inform him she wasn't going to be the rich widow he had been hoping for. "And I also heard the police have a lead on locating Richard."

"What lead?" he snapped.

"Oh, I overheard one of the police officers talking about it when they were at the house asking me about Bill's last words."

Now I had his full attention and this time he couldn't conceal his unease. The last few family members were making their way towards us; he only had a few seconds left to quiz me. He grabbed my arm and led me further away and through a heated whisper said, "Look, this isn't some schoolgirl game. Tell me what you know! What did Bill say?"

I smiled. Finally I had unnerved him and I was in charge. I paused, relishing the moment. The mourners began to surround us now. I shook away his grasp and simply said, "Charles."

I left him standing there disorientated while Terry and Jean hugged me farewell. Then April came up and as she was crying too much to speak, I leaned in to hug her, and she seemed to let go of her previous animosity and hugged back. I reached into my pocket and slipped the envelope of evidence into her large, black shoulder bag. It would be her choice to take it to the authorities.

As the rain became more intense everyone made the final dash to their cars. Ava and Shawn got into the limo, and as I went to join them I noticed only Charles remained standing in the gloom.

For the next few months Ava and I just about coexisted in the house. Avoiding each other wherever we could, I used the excuse that I needed to study for my A levels as much as possible and she had taken to frequenting the new wine bar in town several evenings a week. The only meaningful conversation we had featured Charles. April had indeed taken the evidence I planted to the police; I guess she was so desperate to find Richard. Charles had subsequently been questioned which led the police back to our house. Ava was clueless to the whole affair so couldn't tell them anything. With Bill dead, the business sold and Richard still missing, the police had no further leads to investigate. All they had was Charles, so it was him they put all their efforts into breaking. Of course, he couldn't tell them where the money was because he didn't know, but he did eventually confess to Richard's whereabouts – the bottom of the Blue Forest Lake. It was ironic that Richard should end up there, back in the place this whole dreadful affair had started for him with the Bugatti theft. I imagined his car being winched out of the lake, water cascading out the doors revealing a half decomposed, water-logged body still behind the wheel. Poor April. None of this was her fault, and now little Rosie would have to grow up without her father. It wasn't until Ava read about Charles' confession in the paper that she finally stopped defending him.

Potential purchasers for the property came to view until eventually a Chinese businessman made an offer to buy it. He intended to knock it down and build something to his own design, so the state of the house was immaterial.

My eighteenth birthday passed and although I could now visit Piper unaccompanied, Shawn often came with me anyway, and once or twice Carlos as well. We became quite a close group of four. Piper was delighted with our visits and said it really helped her to keep going. Shawn and I decided to split the half-million between us. As Ava would soon disappear with her half of the house funds, and Billie-Joe and Jane would also have their share it was clear Shawn and I would never receive a penny, so we felt it was only fair for us to keep it. Carlos helped me to use my cash to legally purchase a flat near the college. By the summer my exams were finished, and I was ready for the next phase of my life.

Ava busied herself with visits from auctioneers and house clearance companies as she prepared for moving out. I had told her I was going to live with a friend until I moved into halls in September. She seemed pleased that I had sorted myself out without inconveniencing her. On my final day in High Trees, I cleared out my room and packed my car. Some of the house clearance team were milling about taking the final heavy items of furniture. I wandered around the empty rooms one last time, recalling happier childhood memories that had perhaps escaped my recent thinking. I walked down the long corridor to Bill's old room. Two men were heaving his old heavy desk out. As they manoeuvred past me and away with it leaving me in silence, I looked at the space where it had been. All this time it had blocked access to the sliding doors of the cupboard I had once hidden in as a child. I slid open one side. It was just as the last time I had seen it and concealed myself in between the old box files. I recalled the last thing I had seen when I was hiding there. I slid open the other door and there on top of the files was the wooden box.

My hands were shaking as I slowly took it out and gingerly opened the lid. As the painting revealed itself I took a sharp intake of breath – 'The Forcibly Bewitched' by Goya.

I left the house and got into my car, placing the box carefully on the passenger seat beside me. I would keep this painting forever, this memory of my childhood as a spy. I would hang it on the wall of my new flat, to be a constant reminder that deception can often be right in front of you, and even under the same roof.

CHAPTER 24

Maisie listened attentively as I relived my childhood. Eventually she said, "I'm assuming Pip Hutchings is actually Piper Avery?"

Maisie knew Pip Hutchings like an aunt. "Yes, she was released from prison a little before her full sentence and came to live with me until she got back on her feet. She knows everything and has kept my secret all these years. Uncle Shawn and I, and later of course you, became her family. She severed all connections with her own family after their treatment of her."

"And the painting – where is that now?"

"After I married your father, I couldn't risk having it in the house – he never knew about it – so Pip took care of it."

"So what now? If they discover the painting in the gallery is indeed a forgery, what then?"

"Well I don't really know. I need time to think. Come on, let's go."

We left the restaurant and headed back to the station. The grey London skyline was beginning to dot with coloured sparks of electric light as dusk took over from the day. The air was cold and filled with a misty light rain, yet I felt refreshed to be in the open.

Telling my story to Maisie had made me think of my mother, Ava. After the house sale she had moved near her sister in Cornwall, living out the rest of her life alone, unable to trust another man again. We had seen each other occasionally as she had aged, more out of duty than care. Although I never knew what part, if any, she had played in Bill's death, I could never forgive her betrayal of him. Charles had been convicted and sent to prison for the murder of Richard. His mother, Sal, died of an overdose before his trial. He never confessed to his part in Bill's death but that didn't matter to me; he would never be free again and that was good enough.

Shawn and Carlos didn't stay a couple but have always remained good friends. The four of us still get together for the odd reunion and to reminisce. I don't know what became of April. I hope she managed to make a new life for herself.

We reached the station and located the platform for our train home. Throughout the journey, Maisie sat quietly digesting my confession. I spent the trip thinking about what to do next. By the time we reached our stop, I had made a decision and instead of heading home I took Maisie on the ten-minute detour to Pip's house.

"Happy birthday!" Pip announced as she opened the door and saw us there. She noticed my vacant expression and ushered us inside. "What's up?"

I relayed what had materialised in the gallery that morning, ending with, "I want Maisie to see the painting. In all these years, I have never once worried about being exposed as an art thief, but now, with all the latest technology, who knows? And with a family to protect it's a risk I'm not prepared to take."

Looking surprised but knowing better than to argue with me, Pip just smiled and linking arms with Maisie and me she led us through the hallway and up the stairs. She let us go on the landing and stepped forward towards a closed door. "Are you ready?" she asked us.

It had been years since I had seen the original painting. I had been content with my annual pilgrimage to the gallery to view the forgery. I loved the feeling I had seeing it there whilst no one else around me knew the truth.

The room Pip led us into was only faintly lit. "I had a dimmer switch put in with a special bulb to prevent any light damage to the painting," she informed us. "I keep the curtains drawn most of the time as well."

There it was, hanging beside the bed like any other picture. Even in the dim light it glowed like the most beautiful thing in the world. Of course, I had chosen to study the meaning behind the painting in depth whilst I was at art school, and now the connotation seemed more important to me than ever.

Goya uses the painting to poke fun at those who still believe in witchcraft. The scene is based on a satirical play, 'The Forcibly Bewitched', from 1698. The main character, a priest called Don Camillo, is persuaded that a slave named Lucia has bewitched him, and he must not allow the lamp in her room to go out otherwise he would die. In the painting he is depicted filling the lamp with oil with a look of incredible panic and fear in his eyes. Behind him a picture of dancing donkeys dominates, adding to his crazed mind as well as the humour that is being illustrated.

As I looked at this precious image, it occurred to me that I was the one who had become bewitched, trapped like Camillo in my own world, refusing to accept that this exquisite painting did not belong to me.

"It's time to let it go. Next time we see this painting it will be hanging in The National Gallery."

About the Author

Donna Goold works as a professional artist. She paints uplifting visions of seas and skies bursting with colour and light, as well as dark and mysterious woodlands filled with cryptic clues. *The Childhood of a Spy* is her first novel; a story full of twists and turns that she has created in layers like a painting. She also currently runs a Contemporary Art Gallery, Artwave West with her husband, has two daughters, and lives in Devon.

Before you go

Blue Poppy Publishing is quite small, and we rely heavily on word of mouth to spread the word about our books. Donna Goold would also really appreciate reviews and feedback. So if you enjoyed this book, please take a moment to write an honest review either on our website www.bluepoppypublishing.co.uk – or on Goodreads, or social media. If you happen to have a blog about books that's a bonus. We especially enjoy seeing pictures of our books "in the wild", being enjoyed by readers on the beach or in the garden or in exotic[1] locations. You can tweet us at @BluePoppyPub

---

[1] Exotic in this context doesn't have to mean with a glorious sunset over a beach. If it's far enough away from North Devon it could be the local gasworks or a municipal tip.